OTHER TITLES BY IMPSPIRED

Winter's Breath –
by Polly Richardson-Munnelly

Hotel Multiphobia –
By Henry Bladon

When Moonlight Falls –
By Angelina Der Arakelian

Beginnings –
By Matt Spittles

Circus Town Mammals –
By Robbie Taylor

P.O.N.D –
By John L. Stanizzi

The Blue, Red Lyrae –
By Mehreen Ahmed

Candace Meredith

Dedicated to my beautiful family: my youngest son Jaxon, my middle child and only daughter Lilian, my oldest Paton and my fiancée Todd.

Candace Meredith

Chapter One

She dips the quill in ink she uses to write in a journal. The ink is jet black, and she thinks of it like poison; the good, the bad, and the ugly stain the parchment paper.

The stain is as permanent as her predicament: He is gone.

You went away like the night sky ...

Her journal entry begins. She sits by the fire. She thinks of Christmas. Her back is to the darkness in the room where she writes. He died the year before. Her hand shakes and a single trace of her tear stains her face with mascara.

We were engaged five years before we finally got married...

She is unable to write another word. She drinks from a wine glass; the red is reminiscent of the pool of blood that stained his clothing. His face. They were both in the accident. He perished there while she held his hand. He was suspended between the steering wheel and the seat; his belt made him feel cramped. He turned cold in her hand as the paramedics and the firemen worked to remove the hood to free them from the wreckage. Her heart stopped when they notified her; the surgeons could not repair him. There was a hole in his chest where the windshield had been. The car was like a crumpled piece of tin.

Jo-Jo, he said, *I will always love you ...*

The last she heard was a deep breath before his pupils dilated to an unusual amount of black. She thought she could see stars in them like the entire Milky Way galaxy. She got lost in the moment, like he was pulling her in, before they got to the hospital and she would get the news. She went to the compound where she found the pitiful little sedan – their rental – and wondered what might have been if they had their 4Runner instead.

The boy made a left turn, and we did not have time … before the brakes locked up.

Then there is a knock on her front door. She checks the peep hole to find her roommate standing there. She opens the door...

"Jolene, I lost my key..." she says, and Jolene takes a step back. Her roommate enters the door as she closes it softly.

"It's fine Kim, I wasn't asleep."

Kim is ten years younger than Jolene. They met at the hair salon, both in desperate situations. Kim styled Jolene's hair after the accident. Kim never met Dillon. Jolene needed a roommate in order to keep up the house; Kim needed a place to stay. Jolene offered her a cheap room. Her Beverly Hills home is immaculate, and Kim is in awe of it. She uses the pool and the other amenities. Jolene's husband, Dillon, was a corporate attorney. He was the prosecuting lawyer for the firm that filed suit against the oil company; that was the last case he'd ever win and Jolene didn't need the money – she needed the company, but at the price of some things going missing.

"I would never take anything from you, Jo," Kim has

said and Jolene wants to believe her. She goes away sometimes for overnight stays at the Royal Caribbean where Dillon would take her so they could get away. Dillon was born and raised in California but closer to LA, and Jolene lived in Orange County growing up. They both loved the sun, the beach, the in-ground pool. Jolene would stay there in the suite they shared. She would cry herself to sleep; she tells herself she will not stay anymore, to not cry, and to not leave the house with Kim who hosts parties. Jolene turns forty next year around Memorial Day, and Kim has just turned thirty.

Jolene sits back down to write.

We would have had a baby if I could carry ...

She finishes the entire first chapter after she writes about her three miscarriages, and she closes the book. She stores it away in the drawer at her massive oak desk – her husband's desk – his office. She now uses the space to write her memoir: *Letting Love by the Lake ...*

That part is a secret. A grand ending.

Jolene turns out the light and heads toward her bedroom. She can hear her roommate chatting, likely with Nate, her boyfriend, who surfs the Pacific Coast and works as a Coast Guard. He seems friendly. Mature. But not all their friends seem that way. Jolene thinks about her day tomorrow as she takes a late night shower; she is traveling for work. She is a writer and a photographer. She has started photographing weddings. She thinks of her own wedding; they were married in the fall at her sister's house in Montana. Her sister, Gwyneth, married a rodeo star. His name is Jack. She needs to visit her sister soon. The wedding she will be covering is set for December – a Christmas-themed wedding, but it's not cold enough in Beverly Hills. She knows the fire has died; she enjoys its ambience even if it has no practicality. The flames are the inspiration that heighten her mood for creative inspiration. The wedding is white, red and gold themed aboard a Cruise Liner and set for December 2nd. Jolene is anxious to do her first wedding; she's done baby, high school graduations, and holidays, but this is her first wedding as the widow of Dillon Page. He was well known in Hollywood – the prosecuting attorney for a legal dispute among directors and production rights. The settlement went well and his rise in fame bought the house. Jolene turns the shower off and settles into bed. Her alarm is set for five o'clock in the morning. She is taking pre-wedding photos to get herself content when the wedding is in five days.

At the sound of her alarm she finds she slept well and she lets the dog out; Dillon brought home a French Bulldog weeks before the accident and they named him Cash. She pours wet food into the bowl and adds the dry. She starts the coffee pot. She hears an argument and goes to the porch where she can enjoy the breeze and the ocean out her door. She is traveling to Southern California to Carlsbad where she'll be taking photos of the couple along Coastal Highway – the couple wants photos at the beach before sailing aboard the cruise ship. As she gets dressed, the front door slams and she finds Kim in the kitchen.

"Everything okay?" The silence is awkward.

"Yeah, everything will be fine." Kim pours a mug with coffee.

10

"Alright. I'll be going. Let me know if you need anything."

Kim flashes her a smile. Jolene leaves as Cash returns indoors. She takes off for Southern California where she'll photograph the sun rise. The couple is there early as she pulls into a lot reserved for public parking. She finds Vanessa and Dan who are elegantly dressed; Dan in blue button down and khaki, and Vanessa in a summer dress. Jolene grabs her gear and stages the camera in the cool sand. The air is chilly, but it's still sixty-nine degrees in California. They are photographed looking at and away from the camera; Jolene captures as many natural poses as she can. They hold hands before a purple sky; the scenery cannot be any more beautiful. Jolene counts 100 photos taken; the private photo shoot lasts an hour and she gives them her card. She compiles the photos onto a USB drive and sends them the best she has. The whole affair costs a few hundred and although photography is not paying the bills it buys Cash chewy toys and she's satisfied. She stops by the gas station to fill the 4Runner she thinks about not having during the accident – keeping it only because he loved it so much – and when she turns off Coastal Highway she sees lights in her rearview and realizes she's being pulled over. She triggers her turn signal and pulls off to the side, and when the officer approaches she lets down her window.

"Good afternoon," his voice is in control, in character, for a police officer. His badge says Police Officer Jodi McCain – a state policeman for California.

"Hello, Officer McCain." She musters a smile.

"Do you know why I am pulling you over today?"

"Was I speeding?" She is modest.

"No," he gives her a sideways glance.

"I'm sorry…"

"I've pulled you over on a safety violation … your rear light is out … and your tags have expired."

"Oh, okay…" she is perplexed. "My husband always took care of those things."

"And where is your husband?"

"Beverly Cemetery … he died."

"I'm sorry to hear that." Officer Jodi McCain tears a paper from his notepad and makes his notes, "This will give you a month to get things squared away…" and he tears another, "and this one here is on me."

"Thank you." She takes both folded pieces of paper.

"Have a good day, Miss." He tilts the bill of his bucket hat.

"You, too." She says and winds up the window.

She drives off without looking them over and heads toward the San Diego Gaslamp District where she is meeting a colleague for lunch.

"Old Sorority Sisters," her friend laughs as they enter together and are seated outside.

Jolene tells Vicky of the drive there.

"But whatever does he mean by 'it's on me'?" Her

laugh is infectious.

"I don't know." Jolene sips from a glass of ice water with extra lemon.

"You mean you haven't looked?"

"No, I haven't." Jolene wails and her voice carries.

Vicky has moved back to California following her divorce after a marriage that took her to New York for twelve years.

"What are you waiting for? Open it."

Jolene has both pieces of paper in her purse and she retrieves them as the server approaches.

They both order a salad and are served endless soup and salad with buttered rolls.

Jolene's hands shake as she pulls away at the bit of folded letter.

"It's a notice of violation," she says, and Vicky takes a margarita from the server.

"Any day is a margarita day when you're in California." She laughs. "But go on..." she gestures with her wrist.

Jolene takes the other paper, unfolds it, and on the note is a number.

"A cell number," Jolene says.

"Not just any cell number," Vicky winks, "it's his cell

number."

Jolene doesn't take another look; she folds the paper and tucks it back into her purse.

Vicky chats about a magazine she is developing in the area; her work in advertising in New York pays well and she is set to develop a local magazine on Cruise Life. She invites Jolene to do the photographs for the magazine, and entices her to consider working together. Jolene is impressed with her friend's sincerity, even after not seeing one another for years, but staying connected over social media as time allowed.

"So are you gonna call him?" Vicky's voice chimes in as they receive the bill.

"I don't know." Jolene says casually, "I don't know that I should."

"Oh, why not?" She waves.

"Is it appropriate?"

"And if not? So what…"

Vicky's words stay with her through the night and by morning she thinks about the pending wedding and her plans to visit Montana —and places the note in her bedside table.

As she does each day, she takes out the journal she uses to write her memoir and feels a bit differently but she brushes off the feeling and she begins…

Dillon stole my heart with a proposal on Valentine's Day… although he thought it might be cheesy, he did it because the ring came attached to the most beautiful roses. Then he got on one knee.

Jolene and Dillon were starting life together after college. After graduation with their Bachelor's they went on to law school and a Master's program. Jolene excelled in writing, and her first book *Twist* went on to be represented by a renowned literary agent and was later published to become a NY Times best seller. Jolene hopes for her memoir to help other women who have been widowed, and she plans to release self-help guides after its release. She feels that Vicky's proposal has come at the right time in life; she wants to extend her photography business to include commercial sales. After the wedding photo shoot, she intends to visit her sister and has packed ahead of time. Her nieces Anna and Clara are in high school: one a freshman and the other a senior. She knows they'll be off to college and she won't see them as much. Visiting her sister on Christmas in Montana is like going to the Caribbean in spring; *the snow is wild there*, she thinks. They typically pick her up from the airport with chains on their tires. Gwyneth and Jack include her in the rotation on Christmas morning; Jolene feels special there, and her nieces are the ones who fill the void from not having her own children.

On December 2ⁿᵈ she heads to the wedding that is reserved at four o'clock in the evening. She mingles aboard the cruise ship and they leave port to cruise the Pacific and head out toward Alaska where the groom spent his childhood. Vanessa and Dan's ceremony commences on time, and during sunset their vows are read. Jolene captures more beautiful photos over the sun that is cast in the West. It reminds Jolene of the scene from the *Titanic* as the main cast is filmed among an orange sky. Photos continue into the reception and then again when they port outside of Alaska. The wedding is held over five days during the cruise and there are two hundred guests on the ship; Jolene cannot help but think that wealth has some advantages – not everyone can afford a wedding like this one. They bust their champagne bottle against the bow of the ship and the hundreds applaud them; there is not a moment to miss as Jolene captures every moment.

Chapter Two

"How was the wedding?" Kim asks as they have their morning cup of coffee.

"It was a luxurious and fabulously wealthy wedding." Jolene is triumphant.

"Must be nice," Kim sniggers.

"But what about you? Not everyone gets to do hair and makeup for celebrities."

Kim huffs sarcastically. "What? Like all us cosmetologists get fancy weddings."

"Some might," Jolene shrugs. "By the way, can you watch the house while I go to my sister's?"

"Of course."

"And how about Cash?"

"Oh, he's fine. Let him stay here with me."

Jolene thinks about her decision, but lets it go – she wants to trust Kim. She's a sweet young woman. She takes to the office and finds her husband's files in a drawer. She fills out the appropriate paperwork and attaches a check. She intends to place it in the mailbox before she heads out to meet Vicky; they plan to get a run in. Jolene opens the desk drawer and retrieves the journal and she stencils on its pages…

We were about to arrive at my sister's when he turned left; we were

17

visiting for the holiday, New Years, when we would exchange gifts. We never made it there; I returned home to make funeral arrangements.

She has been through one New Year without him. Both her mom and dad died fairly young. Her father died at age sixty-eight from failed lungs, and their mother at age seventy-seven from cancer. They did have Dillon's family, but they went to his sister's every Christmas in Florida because the weather was warm. Jolene liked the snow; she blamed herself for a while — if only they had not been driving. Jolene won't drive now and she flies instead; she was there in October for Clara's birthday. She is three years older than her sister Anna but both were fall babies — Montana is stunning in the fall. That took them there for the wedding. Jolene met Dillon in college and proposed the year they graduated. On Valentine's Day. They didn't marry until after he graduated law school. Life had been too busy. After law, he opened his own practice in Beverly Hills. They married in Montana among the leaves of color. She thinks about this as Christmas is coming. Her first Christmas without him. A year had gone by in a flash as the days dragged on with each breath she was without him. Dillon was her companion. Her best friend — her best everything. He was funny, kind and smart. She doted on his shoulder over movies. They had pillow fights in the bedroom. Then there were the pregnancies... and the miscarriages. She didn't understand her body. The doctors could not give an answer. She tried artificial insemination and then IVF ... to no avail. She miscarried and the ordeal was causing a strain in their marriage, and at age thirty-nine she got Cash. She thinks about turning forty next year and how he would have a party for her special day... he was a master of surprises. She cannot help but wonder what he would have up his sleeve. Dillon's brother Drake and his wife stay connected … then she wonders too if they would stick around if she met someone new. The thought had never crossed her mind before and then she thought of the number – about Christmas, about the New Year, and she places the letter in the side pocket of her purse and in three hours she'll board the plane.

She meets Vicky as planned and they run along the boardwalk in Santa Monica. Vicky is her ride to LAX – the airport of Los Angeles. They shower at the luxurious hotel where Vicky stays while the home she purchased is renovated. They enjoy a margarita and chat about plans for the holidays; Vicky wants to schedule a date to do Zumba once a week. Jolene would like to do two.

"No problem," Vicky says and they raise their glasses to make a toast of the coming new year when they plan a new life together … one who is divorced and the other a widow – but they have each other. Jolene is happy to have Vicky and her sister.

Upon arrival, she makes her way to the baggage claim and among her things is Gwyneth and Jack; they receive her embrace warmly. Gwyneth is an image of their mother and Jolene takes after her father; Jolene is red, blue eyed, freckles and Gwyneth is blond, curly, dimples and thicker around the hips. Jolene is lean, tall and athletic while Gwyneth is wholesome and warm. They are both beautiful.

"It's so good to see you," Gwyneth says and Jack takes her bags. They walk together into the cold evening air. The flight was delayed from a snow storm. The blanket of thick white powder touches her feet; she is cold. The girls leave the gift shop and meet them outside. Clara is an image of her mother; an image of *their* mother. Jolene misses her parents too; they were always so happy especially when together. Their mother baked on the holidays; Jolene longs for her cakes and sweet tea. But they still have each other. The four wheel drive takes them home; their log cabin is grand. The A-frame is supported by natural wood. Inside the lighting emanates from chandeliers. There are five bedrooms and four bathrooms. Jolene takes the guest room. She empties her bags and hangs them in the closet. As she re-enters the kitchen she finds baked chocolate chip cookies and peach tea waiting for her. With Vicky she drinks wine, but with her sister it's tea – a family tradition. Gwyneth has a wide smile and perfect, porcelain teeth. Jolene wants to be close to family during the pain. She left her journal at home. She thinks she should have brought it. As the girls go to bed, Jolene stays up with her sister and chats about mom and dad. The evening wanes and they too turn in for bed. That night Jolene dreams of Dillon – of seeing his beautiful face without the pool of blood foaming from his chest and onto his face. In her dream he says it again: *I will always love you, Jo,* but this time he isn't smiling; his stern look is something else like when he's had something on his mind. Then she sees him and his body is aglow and from behind him it's as if angels are singing and he steps into this light and he is shrouded in a light of indigo. *I have to go, Jo,* he says to her and she sees his back and when he steps into the light he is gone and she awakens feeling startled – his face, that expression… his departure all seemingly so lucid. She cries knowing it was his time but not hers, and she cannot help but wonder why. She feels in her heart that her memoir is a means for closure.

Wishing she could close it, like a book, and be done with it — not with him, but with the pain. Why was he so serious? She feels deeply that he wants what's best. Did he choose to go? He went into the light because he must, she thinks, and he has never felt so distant, so far away.

That morning she is up early with her sister; it is Christmas Eve. They make breakfast and can smell the pine in the air. They dine on waffles while allowing the others to sleep when Jolene tells her sister of the mysterious officer who left her with his number.

"Why do you think he did it, Jo?" Her sister calls her by her famous nickname.

"What do you think?"

"Well duh," her sister taps her shoulder, "so you'd call him … you know, he said that one was on him…"

"So …"

"So he offered to pay for it…"

"No, get out of here. I'm serious. Look Jo, what else would it mean?"

"I don't know…"

"Well, was he good looking?"

"Well, yes.. I guess, I'd say so…"

"Jo, you know if he looked good or not."

"Yeah, but he had that hat…"

"Oh, come on!"

"Yes, Gwynn, I'd say he was good looking."

"Then you've got to call him."

"What are you ladies discussing?" Jack kisses his wife.

"Jolene got a number."

"A number for what?"

"She got pulled over … and he slipped her a number."

Jack bellows, "He gave you his number? Like as in to call him?"

"Yes." Gwyneth smiles.

Then the girls come downstairs.

"Who gave you his number?" Clara overheard the conversation.

Anna puts eggs on her plate.

"Just some guy …" Jack laughs again, "a cop."

"Well, men are pretty attractive when in uniform," Gwyneth assures them.

"Was he good looking?" Jack pries further.

"She thinks so." Gwyneth doesn't hold back.

"Then call him," Jack says with a mouth full of

bacon.

"Yeah, you should call him," Anna pipes in while filling a glass with almond milk.

They dine over breakfast while back at home Kim and Nate have house guests. It's like the entire brigade arrived at the door. Kim doesn't know how to control the number of guests who are arriving. She does not turn them away. The indoor pool is full, and the guests play pool and cards at the tables. There is alcohol and music. The house is tucked away in the hills but the party erupts outside. A police cruiser shows up at the door.

"We got a noise complaint." The Officer is accompanied by another officer when Kim turns down the music.

"No problem, officer," she says, "we'll be sure to keep it down."

"If we get another complaint you're going in for a public disturbance." He is serious.

Kim waves them off with the music turned down.

"Party poopers." Nate snickers and drinks from a bottle of cold brew. He is thirty-two and invited the entire Coast Guard for his birthday that is in three days.

Back at Jack and Gwyneth's place Jolene sends a text message. The officer pulls out of the driveway and is stopped at a red light when he gets the message.

Call me. He responds and Jolene is shocked to receive

the response so soon.

"Do it." Her sister says, and Jolene takes a deep breath.

"Okay," she says, and she puts the phone to her ear.

"Hello," he says, and Jolene says hello back.

"You may or may not believe where I just was."

"Oh? Where is that?"

"A nice little Beverly Hills mansion… I talked with the responsible party who oversees the house guests …"

"You're not talking about Kim?"

"Then you do know her, and that's certainly what she said her name was."

"How big of a party?"

"I got a noise complaint."

"Oh, God."

"No worries. We got it under control but I did expect to see you there."

"You know where I live?"

"I just happened to remember your address."

"Oh, I see."

Officer McCain is on duty. He asks her to save his number and to get in touch when she arrives back in the hills.

"I will," she says, and she decides not to contact Kim. She tells her sister and brother-in-law of the conversation.

"What a freaking coincidence." Gwyneth is perplexed.

The day turns to evening and the girls open a single gift for Christmas Eve. They receive their favorite brand of hoodie and a pair of jeans. Next they open lip gloss and jewelry, but the rest has to wait until morning. Jolene goes to bed hoping not to dream. She wants utter silence – the deep peace of the quiet. She loves Dillon but her life must go on. She survived. As the twilight turns to the deep night she doesn't awaken until seven o'clock in the morning, and as she heads downstairs she can smell the bacon. They have breakfast before they open their gifts. The girls hurry and scramble under the tree to read the name tags on the gifts. They open clothes, jewelry, makeup, new shoes and accessories. Jack bought his wife pajamas, roses, and a white gold gift set: ring, earrings and a necklace to match. Jolene opens a makeup case, bath set, and Louis Vuitton jacket. She got her sister a Dooney & Bourke purse and a wallet for Jack. She gives the girls their favorite brands of shirts and jeans. Gwyneth told her what to get them. Then she gives each one a purse by Prada. Jolene then thinks of home to which Gwyneth says, "Perhaps it's better to find another roommate." Jolene considers it but doesn't want the hassle of the entire ordeal. She says she's considering moving and selling the house - it's too big for just her anyway, and considering she never had the family she wanted.

"Why not move here?" Gwyneth offers, but Jolene cannot leave the hills of California. Her memories are there and she's attached to the state of California.

"It's just a suggestion," Gwyneth says, and they move on to lunch and cake as the day progresses. Jolene says she'll be returning home after the new year. She continues to stay with her sister through the festivities. As Christmas wanes and the sun gives way to a new day they celebrate the new year at the town hall where Jack gets his prize for best performances; he is a bull rider and owns horses. The log home is surrounded by eighteen acres of ranch style living. Jolene feels warm among them despite the temperatures. The town hall hosts the local bull riding committee and they gamble on the horse raises. *Gold Rush* is their prize winning horse and overall their life is pretty grand. Gwyneth feels for her sister – to lose her husband would be the end of someone so significant and profound in her everyday life. She wishes for her sister's happiness while not being too pushy.

Both girls ride horses and they receive honorable recognitions for their riding techniques. The family is in the limelight and Jolene feels in awe of them; she couldn't be any more proud of the girls or happy for her sister. She shares their love and is pleased to have them during the holidays. They raise a toast with their champagne glasses, and as the ball drops they drink and the hour turns to midnight and they return home to the girls who are in bed. Jolene crashes into the guest room queen bed and drifts off to sleep. In the morning she awakens to a text: *Good morning*, it says and she realizes it's from Officer McCain when another text pops up: *Happy New Year* comes through. She texts back: *Happy New Year Officer McCain...*

Call me Jodi, he texts followed by a wide-smiling emoji. Jolene feels younger again as she sends back a rose aside *okay …*

Have a safe flight home.

Does he know? She thinks. She must have told him. She's so tired and groggy in the morning and her memory is awful. She shrugs.

I'll be flying home at noon (aircraft emoji)

Good thing (winking emoji)

And she doesn't hear from him again until she hugs her sister goodbye and it's Vicky and Jodi at the same time: *What are you doing tonight?*

Sleeping. She responds to both of them.

Vicky: *Get some good rest*

Jodi: Crying emoji

And she lands safely at LAX and she goes to her car that is stationed there and when she returns home she can smell the fragrant salty air. And her house is a wreck. Through the front door she finds Kim on the sofa surrounded by beer. The house stinks of alcohol. She nudges Kim, "How was the party?" But it's as if she is dead. Jolene turns to the mantle that is decorated for Christmas and notices a large crystal egg missing from above the electric fireplace. She walks toward it and it's gone. She moves to her bedroom and the bed sheets are ruffled; she doesn't leave an unkempt bedroom. Someone was in her bed. She moves to her dresser and her jewelry box is missing. She sends a disgruntled text to Jodi McCain: *I've been robbed.* He responds almost immediately: *Do you want to write a report?*

Ugh, she says in a reply.

I'll be over to get the report.

Okay.

Jodi appears at her place and as she gives him the news he explains that she cannot report a break-in since the roommate is allowed to live there.

"But to get her out you must file a report."

"What kind of report?"

"Destruction of property. Failure to pay rent. Something like that. Start an eviction notice."

Jolene hesitates. She is too kind. She signs the report anyway and files for an eviction due to destruction of property.

"I'll get to this right away," Jodi says and she simply says, "Thank you."

"And you're not sleeping tonight too are you?"

"Well, not until later."

"How about six o'clock? I'm off duty then."

"Where would you like to meet?"

"Risorto's ... an Italian place downtown..."

"Sure. I like Risorto's …"

"See you there around seven then."

"Okay, I'll see you there."

He nods and she closes the door. Kim is still unconscious and Jolene huffs. The house is a disaster and she thinks it's time to sell – but all her memories with Dillon are in the house. Then she thinks too about her dream … about his words … *Jolene I have to go.* Was that a sign?

Chapter Three

They meet at the Italian joint at seven. He is clean cut, shaved and smells of cologne. He wears blue jeans and a collared shirt. He orders the spaghetti while Jolene orders the vegetable lasagna. When they receive their food she watches his careful movements; even his mannerisms are clean and precise; he cuts his pasta and twirls it with a fork. She enjoys a red wine while he has ice water. They chat casually about where they're from and share some experiences of the past. He had a brother who went insane; been locked up in an asylum, but he omits the crime he committed. Jolene did not want to pry; he didn't want to get into details. She shares stories of childhood in California and how Gwynn met Jack at the rodeo where her sister was attending a bachelorette party. Jack was the brother of the groom. She speaks of Christmas and how her husband died last year suspended behind the wheel of the car.

"Did he serve any time?" He asks of the young boy who made the left turn.

"He was only twenty," she says, "he was young and scared."

"So you didn't file charges?"

"No."

"Is that a habit of yours?"

"But you have to understand."

"Oh I do, I know how accidents happen."

She takes a bite of lasagna, and he smears butter bread across his pasta sauce. She understands through his silence that he upholds the law – but she has a soft heart. The lighting there is dim and the restaurant is sparsely filled. She speaks of writing and her first published novel. She talks of the memoir "still just a journal" that she is writing. He listens and smoothly talks her into a shared dessert: a molten chocolate cake with fudge, brownie and syrup. They eat from the same plate. He is charming. She is beautiful. She wears a slim red dress accentuated by red hair. Her hazel eyes look green in the lighting. After he pays the bill they head to the beach. They remove their shoes and walk barefoot in the sand. He talks some more about his mother who was a hard case in her youth, how she favored his brother, and how she went into rehab never to come out.

"Clayton is just the same," he says.

Jodi, like Jolene, lost the only family he had. Jolene doesn't know what to say. She is careful not to ask too much. She lets him speak of them in the way he is comfortable. She has missed her parents for years – evidently his father wasn't around and his mother had numerous relationships but none to last. Jodi is forty-two, never married, but had a long relationship that lasted a decade but she met another and moved on. Her name was Alayna, but again he spares her the details. They talk into the night when he holds her hand.

"What do you think about seeing one another again?" He asks with turquoise-green eyes winning her over.

"Sure." She is polite, "When?"

"I'm off duty every night at six ... just let me know."

"I have a pretty flexible schedule..."

"We've talked a lot but I forgot to ask what you do."

"My husband left me a life insurance policy ... but I also write and I do photography."

"Ah. What, stories?"

"Yes. I write fiction. But lately I'm working on a memoir."

"What about if you don't mind me asking?"

"A memoir mostly about widowhood."

"I see."

"It's only been a year..."

"Let me know if I'm too ... cheeky ..." he smiles.

"I would never say you're too cheeky." They laugh together.

She goes home. She thinks about her memoir but leaves it until the morning. She crawls into her king-sized bed and snuggles into the covers.

"I love you." She whispers into the night. "I will always love you." Then she dreams. She dreams that Jodi is drowning and she awakens and turns on her light. Something is amiss. She feels disoriented like she needs to write. She only knows what should be her next chapter ...

and when she heads into her husband's office she pulls the drawer to find it empty.

"Where are my journals?" She asks aloud for only Cash to hear.

"Where the hell are my journals?" She asks aloud down the hallway. Then she knocks furiously on Kim's door.

Kim opens the door groggily. "What?" She yawns.

"Your damn party, Kim," she's exasperated. "My journals... all of them... missing."

"I'm sorry, your what?"

"My fucking journals, Kim! All of them. I use them to write my memoir."

"I'm so sorry..."

"I began those journals when Dillon died."

"I'm sorry, I don't know..."

"No one is ever allowed in that room, Kim."

"Then who went in?"

"You tell me!"

"Well, the police ... when they did the walk through... that's all I know."

"A walk through for what?"

"Narcotics, I guess."

"And?"

"And? They found nothing… I promise."

Jolene closes Kim's door. *Someone must have thought they'd make money off a published author,* she thinks. She goes back to bed feeling defeated. *The shit never ends,* she tells blank space and closes her eyes only to drift off into reverie.

"You can always start new ones," Kim tries to be friendly in the morning.

"Imagine always starting over again," Jolene says then moves out of the kitchen to take a shower. While bathing in the warmth of the cascade she considers a long vacation. She has plans with Vicky today and she starts to concentrate more on the present moment. They are meeting at a vegan restaurant that opened in the area. Jolene prefers vegetables over meat. Her physique is strong and contoured. Vicky strives to do the same. They meet at the restaurant for brunch just before eleven o'clock.

"Oh, that bitch," Vicky says of Kim.

"She's not in the right here," Jolene remains calm.

"No, definitely not."

Jolene decides to change the subject. She tells Vicki about Jodi … including the walk through when she was not home.

"That's a coincidence," she responds, "but you know they didn't find drugs … did they?"

"She says no and he didn't mention anything."

Vicki eats from a leafy green salad and Jolene has tofu over spinach. The sky out their window looks opaque.

"Looks like rain," Vicky says, "but about the magazine ... can you cover Cruise Life Cuisine?"

"For you, anything. How is that coming along?"

"It's ready. But I need some writers still if you come across any..." Vicky winks.

"What would you like me to write about?"

"Anything. New trends. The content is up to you. I'm open."

"I'll cover the band. Entertainment. That sort of thing."

"And food." Vicky raises her glass.

"And food." Jolene gives her a toast with her glass and they sip wine before paying the check.

As they are parting Jolene gets a text: *Busy?* It's from Jodi.

Just leaving from brunch, she replies. She feels anxious to ask Jodi of the walk through wondering why he hasn't mentioned anything.

Want a date tonight? He responds.

I'm covering a Cruise tonight, for a magazine, the food, band, entertainment, that sort of thing...

Too bad, I'd like to see you.

Then meet me there.

You can do that?

I'm doing this for a friend.

Then I'll be there.

She sends an emoji. *It's a date.* She says simply: *okay.*

She gets started by first locating the band: *Dwayne & Kasey* are a male and female duet. They will be attending the next cruise that is set for Saint Martin that week. She interviews them both; they are a married couple who met overseas in Europe and discovered one another's voices. They have been touring for five years. Jolene is pleased with the article. They are an attractive couple; in the next hour Jodi should be there. She is happy. The evening is a bit cool so she covers her shoulders with a shawl. She covers the menu selection next: an array of seafood covers the inside along with a lavish buffet, appetizers, platters and drinks. Her goal is to entice local residents and beyond to book a cruise. Jolene wonders if Vicky has connections with the ship owners. She believes the connections are from her advertising background and the magazine is certainly a form of advertising. She enjoys making connections with long ago friends and wonders what she would do without her, then a hand brushes her shoulder and she turns to find Jodi who has found her in the dining area as she hovers above the menus.

"Find anything good?" He hands her a solitary yellow rose. "From my garden."

"Your garden?" She smiles.

"It's from outside my condo really." He is charming.

36

"Thank you." She isn't abashed.

She finds the front table where the chefs put out platters for photographing. She uses her digital camera and captures close images of beautiful dishes.

"This is a good start to the magazine." Before thinking first she blurts out, "I'm going to be away for a week on the cruise liner ... not sure if you want to..."

"Want to join you?"

"That's what I'm asking."

"When?"

"It's next week."

He nods, thinking for a moment.

"I'll try my best ..." he shines like stars in his eyes.

"I know it's last minute so I understand ..."

"I'll let you know my room number when I get there..."

She gazes at his expression which is serene, calm.

"Okay." She says in response to his confidence.

They watch the twilight as the day turns to evening. They gaze at the stars. When her photographing feels complete they walk off the cruise liner and he walks her to her car. She drives home in silence. She drives past Dillon's grave. She names a star after him near Orion's Belt and when she arrives home she searches the house. She wants those journals back precisely where she left them – but they are not there. She takes Cash outside and decides to walk beneath a blanket of the starry night sky. She walks to the graveyard and finds Dillon near a palm tree. She has a single yellow rose and she lays it down.

"I know you would want the best..." she cries lovingly... "I hope you would approve. He seems like a good guy."

She feels a drizzle and waits in the rain. She makes her way back home beneath a deluge. Cash shakes his fur as they re-enter the indoors and she stops in the mud room and removes her jacket. She takes her phone from her pocket and sends the text: *You never told me you did a walkthrough of the house.*

His response was quick: *We didn't find anything.*

Where did you look?

Where there were guests.

The office?

I'm not sure. Not that I can remember. Why?

My journals are missing.

Do you want to add them to the list of stolen/ missing on the report?

I mean they're gone.

I'll add them to the report.

Okay.

They say no more, but Jolene feels betrayed. Lost. But in the morning, she finds Kim packing.

"You are leaving?" Jolene is not surprised.

"Nate has a place for us." She is happy.

"Okay." Jolene is feeling empty.

"You won't be alone? Right?"

"I've met someone but we're not rushing."

"It's good to take your time... I mean with being widowed and all..."

"Right." Jolene is done. She tosses her hand in the air. "Let me know if you need help." She maintains composure.

"Thanks." Kim goes back to packing and Jolene does the same, uncertain who will watch Cash during her leave so she takes to the internet and locates pet sitters in the area; there are many, she finds Susan's Sitting and leaves a message. It is Friday and she will be taking a cruise to Saint Martin in three days. The cruise lasts seven days and she is to interview the guests for first hand experiences aboard the liner for the magazine. She wants to enjoy her time there and she wonders if she is doing right by inviting Jodi; she thinks too – how can it hurt? As the days pass and she prepares for her trip they communicate over text and he finally verifies he can be there.

I've got room 7, his text says as she boards the cruise ship.

I'm 27.

She has a room to herself. She's grateful to have company but she doesn't want to bore him. She settles into her room and wants to capture the nightlife on a cruise liner first thing. They meet in the dining hall; he looks good. He is formal and she chose to wear a long black dress. They find a table together. She places a cloth napkin across her lap.

They order shrimp and the fish of the day: flounder and a side of scallops. Jolene receives a classic Caesar salad before her meal. She drinks sweet red wine. He has a beer.

"Oh my god…" they hear a voice over them.

He turns to look but he already knows that voice.

"Jodi … how the hell can you afford to be here?"

His face is flush.

"Alayna," he says, "hello." She doesn't get another word in, "Jolene, this is my ex Alayna." "And I'm her husband Rick," he steps forward. They shake hands.

"I'll ignore you've asked that."

"Well, aren't you still a cop?"

"I am."

"I own this ship," Rick is entirely wealthy… and charming. "Let us know if we can get you anything at all."

"I'm covering this ship tonight for an emerging magazine…"

"Is that right? What magazine?"

"Cruise Life... my very good friend started the magazine. She's moved back to California from New York. She's in advertising."

"Be sure to cover the live entertainment this evening."

"I sure will." Jolene smiles.

"The name is Rick Boyd... what would you like to know for the magazine?"

"Honey, can't this be done later?" Alayna is impatient.

"No, it'll only be a minute ... go mingle with guests and I'll catch up with you."

Rick has jet black hair and blue eyes. He is tall but not too thin ... almost a Clark Kent appearance. Their food is served and he tells them how he invested, how he bought the cruise liner and how he plans to build more. Jolene has a "from the beginning" story for the magazine. Then she sees Vicky coming toward them; she's wearing a flashy gold dress.

"Hey," Jolene waves. "We've just met Rick Boyd, owner of this ship."

"And you are?" Rick asks.

"Vicky is owner of the magazine."

"Oh, that will make a great headline," Vicky says, and she asks for a photo for the magazine. She flashes a quick one with her phone.

He is valiant. "I should get back to my wife." He says, "It

was nice to meet all of you. I'm sure you'll do a good job marketing my work."

"We sure will." Vicky smiles a toothy grin.

Rick nods and walks away.

"Why didn't you mention you'd be here?"

"Last minute decision," she says, "who's the new catch?" She winks.

"Hello," Jodi says.

"Vicky, this is Jodi."

He shakes her hand. He wipes his lip with the cloth napkin.

"It's nice to meet you."

"Same here." He takes a bite followed by a little water. When the server approaches Jodi orders a draft beer and Jolene tells Vicky to sit down.

"I don't want to intrude…"

"Nonsense, you can help us decide what to cover tonight."

"Let's do poker night." Vicky orders a martini.

"Definitely. The casino and the live entertainment like Rick said…" Jolene looks to Jodi, "Rick's wife happens to be Jodi's ex."

"Oh? Small world," Vicky says.

"It is." Jodi has an equally charming smile.

Chapter Four

Jolene travels behind as they enter the casino. She asks if guests' photos can be taken. They oblige, most of them. She sees Alayna mingling with girlfriends; they are flashy, showy. She approaches without hesitation; Jodi goes to the men's room.

"Can I have your photographs ... for the style portion of the magazine?" Jolene asks and Alayna darts her eyes toward her guests.

"Her friend started a magazine," she says and they laugh heartily.

"Then let her take a photo," a brunette says.

Jolene's flash brightens the room. No one else seems to notice. The guests are into their own hand upon the table. The brunette's husband approaches and he's significantly older. Jolene wonders if the twenty year age difference is genuine. She learns that he owns a few casinos in Vegas and invests wisely in oil; his father before him owned tobacco plantations; they are a legacy of wealth. Jolene is comfortable among them; her belated husband had many relationships that were like them. She doesn't speak of her husband. Alayna doesn't mention her ex. She merely brushes her manicured nails through her hair. She notices Jodi looking for his dinner date.

"I think he's looking for you over there," Alayna flicks her nails.

"I better be going then." Jolene is charming and Alayna isn't amused. She takes off toward the band where Jodi is standing and Vicky joins them. They are destined for the Caribbean where they'll port for a day before the cruise ship leaves again – toward home. They enter the evening air together and join the night life at the exquisite top floor pool, gymnasium and other amenities.

"We should get in," Jodi says, and Jolene finds him charming.

"At night?" Vicky muses.

"Why not?" Jodi chimes, "can't get sun burnt this way."

Vicky shrugs, "Then let's get our suits on." She is all smiles.

When they return to the pool it is ten o'clock in the evening. The pool doesn't close until two o'clock in the morning for cleaning and maintenance. Jodi wears Hawaiian swimming trunks. He orders a Bahama Mama for Jolene and drinks another draft beer.

"Vicky, how about you? Can I get you anything?"

"Oh, sure sweet stuff! Give me the Blue Hawaiian Margarita."

"You got it!" And he rushes off; the bar is getting busy.

"He may not be wealthy like the ones you see here," she motions over her shoulder, "but he sure is dreamy."

"He is isn't he?" Jolene beams.

The pool isn't packed like the hot tub. There are young couples soaking up the heat.

"Can you imagine being that young again?" Vicky says, as Jodi returns with a Blue Hawaiian in hand.

"Well, that was quick," Vicky says, and is the first to enter the water.

There are strobe lights across the water; Jodi muses that his hand looks electric blue. Jolene dazzles in a black and silver-studded bikini and Vicky sports a red one piece. Alayna takes notice and stubs up her nose. They are having fun while her company talks progress on investing; those conversations are not for Jolene, and she spots Alayna, wondering if money makes up for the look of boredom across her face. Then she notices Jodi whose eyes are on her; she grins and he smiles back at her; there is a mutual physical, sexual attraction between them when they hear...

"Holy hell, if it's not Jodi McCain," the voice says.

"Well hell, right back at ya Gregory Mann."

They slap a high five.

"Sorry ladies," Jodi muses, "this is my old frat mate ..."

"You were in a fraternity?" Vicky marvels.

"We were, then at the academy together."

"This guy right here," Gregory slaps his shoulder, "best guy on earth."

"What fraternity?" Jolene is amused.

"What did you study in college?" Vicky chimes in.

"Criminal justice... then the academy. Worked in investigation," Gregory says.

"Then I left the investigative work and got another degree in a whole new field. Been building ever since. You still in with the state police?"

"I am." Jodi extends his hand to Jolene... "And this is my date Jolene, and her good friend here, Vicky."

"Two ladies with you, you stud!" They have a laugh.

"Get in the water ..." Jodi jokes and splashes slightly.

"Maybe," Gregory says and he finishes his beer.

"What has you here?" Jodi pries.

"I'm with my wife's family. They come here for a week every year."

"I see."

"They want to try some slots at the casino ... maybe we can catch up later."

They shake in a strong fist hold; their biceps are cut strong and sleek.

"Just another way the world is small," Jolene says.

Vicky nods, "Maybe a little too small at times." She laughs.

"You got that right." Jodi finishes his beer. After several hours in the pool and back to the casino they check in, and Jolene, along with Jodi, walk hand-in-hand toward room number 7.

"Is it time to turn in?" Jodi says and he places one hand on the wall and the other smoothes her face.

"I still have time," she whispers.

He unlocks the door and takes her by the hand and then off her feet. There is a large king size bed covered in red velvet; he got a master suite. Briefly she wonders how he could afford it, but as he lays her down he kisses her so passionately she forgets to care. They take off one another's clothes and he holds onto her with a single thrust and she enjoys the penetration. She breathes into him and her head goes back; he kisses her neck – his hands to her face and he slightly pulls her hair; she moans. They hold tightly onto one another and their skin is smooth and their hair is slightly wet. They change positions and feel one another's bodies; they give into one another completely and when they are spent they fall asleep until morning almost turns to noon and he orders breakfast in the room.

"Sorry to sleep so late," she says and he hands her a white robe from the bathroom. She puts it on and he hands her a breakfast tray for bed. She dines on fruit, yogurt and a pancake.

"You were incredible …" he says, "if you don't mind me saying …"

"You felt good too," she says, and swallows a little orange juice.

"What's on the agenda today?" He asks knowing she

has covered a lot.

"I've already covered the band..."

"The food ... the casino ... the owner and his wife."

She giggles.

"How about your friend?"

"I'm sure we'll see him again."

"And with Vicky ... we can have a nice dinner party."

"True." He winks when they hear a knock on the door.

"Room service," a gentle maid says as he opens the door. She brings him fresh linen and he takes some towels.

"What do you say to a soak in the hot tub?" He asks as the maid leaves.

"Maybe tonight. I'm going to have a shower after we finish up breakfast."

He walks toward her and kisses her subtly and she kisses him back.

After breakfast, she goes to her room and the shower feels divine down her back. She never thought about dating a cop – but who does? Those who dream of a man in uniform?

Jolene and Jodi meet up with Vicky in the casino; they call

for Gregory over an intercom and when they find him he is laughing. Jodi and Gregory man-hug with a slap on the back. Gregory introduces Jodi to his wife, Elaine, and they greet one another with a shake and warm smiles. Jolene asks his background and why he, or they, made the decision to travel on this particular cruise liner.

"Because it's the best especially for all the amenities," Elaine says (considering they go every year). They also chat about their move to California ten years ago. Jodi and Gregory tell Jolene of their last time chatting via online media and then lost a connection.

"Life gets in the way," Gregory says of the time he's been married. Jolene is most surprised by the accident; Gregory survived a motorcycle accident.

"Never take a moment for granted," he says, and Jolene speaks about her marriage and widowhood.

"How unfortunate," Elaine is earnest, as she covers her mouth with her fingertips. They speak of how Jolene met Jodi, that which she calls serendipity but speaking of a fortunate accident now feels inappropriate; she wasn't thinking before. She says now it's fortunate for her to meet Jodi and they talk about Kim and Nate and how they love to host parties. Jodi says the worst of the situation is missing her journals – her life story is in those pages.

"It's awful to have a roommate who steals from you," Elaine says when they are finally seated for a cocktail at the barroom table. They order mixed drinks, and Vicky has been listening intently when she points out that Alayna is coming their way.

"What? No way," Gregory says. "This cruise just keeps getting weirder and weirder!"

"You know her?" Elaine questions as Alayna approaches their table.

"Jodi's old college girl," he says silently.

"Ah," Elaine's eyes meet Vicky's.

Vicky shrugs.

"I recognize you," Alayna darts her finger.

"Likewise, here too..." Gregory bellows. "What brings you on the ship?"

"Her husband owns this ship," Vicky muses.

"You need to get a story on that!" Gregory guffaws and Jodi is amused.

"Is there a story in here, too?" Alayna wonders.

"How cruises bring people together," Jolene says.

"That it does," Alayna rolls her eyes slightly. "Whether we want it to or not," she laughs.

The rest are not amused, but together in a group, Jolene asks for a photo and Jodi sneers, shaking his head but the adult in him joins the photo. Jolene has her final story for the magazine *Cruise Life*.

When Jolene returns home, she finds that Kim has moved out. She is thankful there wasn't confrontation. She heads into her husband's office...

"I don't understand it," she tells Jodi, "I don't let anyone in this room."

"Perhaps you forgot to lock it?"

"Well no, actually I never lock it; I just keep the door closed and off limits."

He looks at her in a sideways glance.

"I know," she huffs, "don't look at me like that."

He shakes his head.

"You don't seem as concerned about the rest of the property."

"Those journals were my blood, sweat and tears."

"I hope you feel okay making new memories."

"I do." She says, "I do."

The next day she is writing the stories for the magazine. The house is big and empty. She can hear her own breathing in isolation when Kim walks in.

"Kim?" She says, "Feeling hopeful."

"I am here to return your key and to apologize again that your things went missing." Behind her Nate joins them, "Tell her the rest," he says defensively.

"Nate doesn't feel anyone he knows would take your things …"

51

"Especially some journals," he says, "that's just weird."

"But they are gone … and coincidentally you had a party…"

"But there was that cop…" Kim says, as she eyes Nate.

"He came back. Not in uniform. Said he left something in that room… I swear no one else went into that room."

"Do you know that officer's name?"

"No, we don't have a name," Nate says, "He wore a ball cap and tee-shirt. Blue jeans. Pretty basic."

"Black hair. Green eyes. Really beautiful skin."

Nate turns to Kim.

"I'm just saying…" she says.

"What did he leave in this room?"

"We don't know…" Nate looks flustered, "Kim let him in…"

"I wasn't thinking," she says defensively.

Jolene is lost for words; she is able to describe Jodi without having met him. She feels disgruntled and believes it seems out of character for him — but how well does she know him? She doesn't except he seems so genuine and courteous. She brushes it off — but what about the jewelry and the crystal that was taken? And what did he leave in that room? Jolene ponders everything in that instant as Kim places the door key upon the desk.

"Thank you, Kim." Is all she can say.

She knows she spoke to him on the phone after the incident. Did he go back inside the house after their conversation? She is bewildered and annoyed. He never mentioned going back inside the house. What is he omitting by not talking about it? She picks up her cell phone and types, *gotta talk,* to which he simply responds *I'm all ears.* She can't believe he could take anything.

Chapter Five

They meet at the Mexican restaurant where she has invited him for dinner. He orders the taquitos de pollo and she has the enchiladas. They are served chips and salsa. Jolene decides to be direct because she knows no other way.

"Jodi," she looks him in the eye, "Kim tells me you went back to the house... out of uniform, and stated you left something in my home, that you had to go back to find it ... specifically in my office."

He uses a cloth napkin to wipe his lip. "Jolene, I was never in your house without a uniform."

"They both say you went back. That you went into the office without your uniform on."

"Both who?"

"Kim and her boyfriend, Nathan. He goes by Nate."

"I can guarantee you the story is fabricated, and no one other than those two and their friends went into that room."

"So they're just lying?"

"You know how many lies I hear in a day? A crack addict lying about the crack being in the car... the false phone call about the boyfriend beating a girl ... the downright lies about not holding a child hostage."

"I see your point."

"So yes, I'm saying they're flat out lying."

"They described you, how you look."

"In uniform …"

"Blue jeans. Tee-shirt."

"Well, there you have it … I don't wear tee-shirts. Only when I'm at the gym … and certainly not on any ordinary basis; and besides, I went back to the station to file the report after I spoke with you. Not back to your house." He snickers.

"Okay, point taken," she says. He is wearing blue jeans but with a collared shirt and not a tee-shirt. He's not boyish and looks honest to her. She dismisses the idea and they chat about Kim and how she's had parties in the past but she never saw anything taken. Jolene confesses she's finally ready to sell the house. He talks briefly about his condo and how it's a perfect space for only one; she agrees her home is too big, it appraised for over two million.

"You'll be set for life if you sell it and downsize," he says and she agrees.

They chat about the magazine and her hopes that Vicky finds more writers and photographers than just herself.

"I don't want to live a cruise life," she muses.

"No, not permanently." He agrees.

They enjoy their Mexican cuisine and he rubs her hand.

"You have nothing to worry about," he says, and she feels warm to the touch. The outside air is warming as spring is near – only a day away from the first day of spring, and the sunny palm beach is beautiful. They take a walk in the sand; it is Saturday and they enjoy Santa Monica. He recommends they look at houses so she can get an idea of what she might like. She says she wants a basic three bedroom and two bath. He enjoys her modesty despite all her money. They get along well and they mesh; something she thought would never happen again after Dillon died. They explore Rodeo Drive, they tour Hollywood, they visit Universal Studios and the days pass by; the birds are soaring above and the dolphins are noticeable from the beaches. They fill one another's day – fill one another's void. They visit Vicky and swim in the pool. They dine at fine dining and BBQ at home. She visits his condo and they swim there, too. They put her house up for sale and the realtor has it listed; in two days there is an offer and she accepts it. They move her things into a storage facility and she lives in a rental until she decides on a home. She completes the entire first magazine for Vicky and it goes to print. They take Cash for walks and gaze at the stars. She tells him of the star she named Dillon and they visit his grave. She holds his hand – she believes she has his best wishes. She buys him yellow carnations and his stone is brightened. She feels fulfilled and in awe of him. She loves him – she has never said it. When they get to the condo they crash into the bed together feeling spent. They love deeply and this he tells her over her shoulder and into her ear. She turns over to face him.

"I do, too." She says softly.

"What?" He holds her close.

"I love you, too." She laughs. They laugh. And they fall asleep into the night and wake the next day. He is making breakfast and Cash is drinking from a food bowl. She emerges wearing a silk robe that is red with white and gold trim. She takes a seat at the center island and they eat fresh fruit, waffles and danishes. He is lavish for her; she completely and entirely dotes on him. When she opens the sugar bowl she finds a ring -- a real beautiful gem. He proposes on the balcony overlooking the Pacific Coast during sunrise.

"Of course, yes," she says. They are only six months into dating, but she feels there is no other answer. They are in love together – and how much more should someone wait to know they are in love? He slides the ring on her finger and she gleams; the most beautiful square cut diamond shines in the sunlight. They embrace and kiss passionately. There is an aura of an exuberant yellow among them. Cash makes his way onto the balcony and Jolene hugs him. She could cry but holds back; he grunts to be petted. Vicky chimes in with a text and Jolene snaps a photo – presses send. Vicky is quick to write back: *Congratulations,* the text says with red heart emojis following after. Then Vicky responds with a place she might like – if she gets there soon – there is an open house and they pencil in a date to meet while Officer Jodi McCain prepares for work, and they kiss again.

Jolene meets Vicky at the open house; the curb appeal is beautiful; there is a lush garden, an outdoor pool and three bedrooms with two baths. The upkeep is minimal and the inside is sleek and modern; there are chandeliers and bling on the walls; the master bedroom is spacious and the en-suite is massive – the walk-in closet is even bigger. Jolene is astonished at the purchase price of eight hundred-fifty-thousand. There is a garage and a small putting green.

"This house is going to sell quick," Vicky says.

"I'm in love," Jolene says, and at the end of the visit she phones Jodi because she wants to put in an offer. He arrives home at eight o'clock in the evening and she shares the listing with him. Going over the photos she shows him the grand space, and he likes what he sees. She shares with him the offer she made: a little over nine-hundred thousand because she knew there would be multiple offers. She waits excitedly and a week later she finds out her offer is accepted and she leaps into Jodi's arms. Then she sends a message to Vicky: *thank you,* it says and she is now a proud homeowner of a house in Orange County. Three weeks later she moves her items from storage to the house. She's on a new journey and she is feeling fulfilled. In the May sunshine there are flowers. Once settled, Vicky hosts a house-warming party at her place. They have mutual girlfriends and the men are invited; it's an occasion for Vicky to serve martinis. They make use of the pool, the drinks and order carry out. They are served Mediterranean wood-fire pizza and garlic bread. Jolene opens gifts: towels, candles, cookware, and a dining set from Vicky.

"Here's to starting over," Vicky raises her glass.

"Perfect," Jolene says and they toast over wine and cheese. The occasion is spent in the company of friends. Jodi pulls Vicky aside and they discuss her fortieth birthday that is two weeks away; he wants it to be a surprise. He asks for Gwyneth's information and Vicky is happy to give him her number; he is hopeful that she can fly in on a short notice. Vicky sends her a message since she inquired to have her at the house-warming party.

Gwyneth texts back: *Sorry I missed the party and I sure don't want to miss her fortieth birthday bash!*

Jodi whispers that Jolene is coming and he follows up with a quick text: *It's Jodi, Jolene's fiancée ... hoping to meet you at the party!*

Gwyneth replies: *Can't wait! When & where? It'll be at Jolene's May 30th, Memorial Day. She's only expecting a cookout but the rest is up my sleeve.* Followed by a winking emoji.

"She's only expecting five of us for the cookout," he says to Vicky before Jolene catches up to them.

"What are you all up to?" She's suspicious.

"I asked Jodi to help with dessert," Vicky says and waves them into the kitchen, "come on in."

"You all do too much." Jolene is modest.

"Nonsense. This is what friends are for!"

They collect the pies, cupcakes and baked cookies and take them outside to be served to the guests. The party lasts until evening when they are all spent. Jodi drives Jolene home to her place and helps her bring the gifts into the house. He spends the night and wakes early in the morning for his shift. He takes a look at the desk where the journal was stored thinking that it's odd for anyone to steal a bundle of journals from the drawer. He leaves quietly, understanding the crystal and the jewelry being taken, having monetary value, but the journals don't make sense. He spends four hours patrolling in his cruiser when the call comes across the radio: woman and a man reported to be in fatal condition off Sunset Boulevard. He responds quickly to the call and arrives on the scene within fifteen minutes; a small two door coupe has collided with a semi; the scene looks terrifying, but as Officer McCain approaches he finds Kim lying in shards. Her boyfriend Nate is suspended behind the wheel. The medics tend to them, cutting them free of the debris and metal, then another officer approaches, "We have Kimberly Anne Turner and Nathan Emory Michaels at the scene," he radios in another officer to help divert the traffic to the left shoulder. "We found some paraphernalia," the other officer says as the semi-trailer driver is taken from the scene in an ambulance.

"From which vehicle?" Officer McCain responds.

"The truck driver. Appears high on cocaine."

"How about the other two?"

"In critical condition but nothing on them. Didn't seem to be paying attention… the driver of the rig says they cut right in front of him; he tapped the bumper and the car spun out and lost control."

"Keep me posted," Jodi says as he steps into the police cruiser and the accident is cleaned up over an hour.

Jodi wants to tell Jolene in person. He finishes his double shift that ends at eight o'clock in the evening. Before responding to her call he phones into the hospital; the only update for both accident victims is critical condition; he takes the news back to Jolene. She is both shocked and saddened. She doesn't want Kim to die and she has a flashback of Dillon behind the wheel too; the accident is eerily similar. *The darker side of serendipity*, she thinks. The following morning she takes to the hospital as Jodi begins his shift. She finds Kim in a bed with tubes and lines. She is on life support; she is in a coma. She has brought flowers and places them on the bedside table.

"Kim," she speaks out loud, "I want you to stay. Please do not leave."

Kim is unresponsive and is breathing through tubes when Jolene hears someone behind and she turns to find Jodi still in uniform.

"I'm just coming to check on you." His voice is low. He places a hand to her shoulder.

"Nathan didn't make it, Jo," he says using her nickname for the first time.

"That's what my husband used to call me."

"Kim does, too," he says and looks pleasantly at her.

"Yes, she does," Jolene whispers.

"They found something in the trunk of the car... I just wanted to tell you when you were ready."

"My journals?"

"No ... a receipt. From a pawn shop. For a large crystal egg."

"Oh. I see." Jolene is disappointed. "Why couldn't she just tell me if she needed the money?"

Jodi shakes his head in silence.

"Well, I still don't wish her dead." She sighs.

"No, of course not," he says, rubbing her shoulder. "Just keep in touch and let me know how you're doing."

"Okay," she says and he walks out of the room. All she can think about is that Kim is without Nate in the same way she lost Dillon. Jolene leaves the hospital feeling that familiar lost feeling she had when Dillon died. She sends Kim a quiet prayer. She visits Dillon's grave. She tells him all she can about Kim. About Jodi. The air is dry, the sun is out and overall the day is beautiful. She looks up to the clear blue sky and feels her prayers were answered; Kim and her boyfriend Nate were not honest people. She takes a deep breath. She leaves his grave feeling sullen and relieved at the same time. She pulls away in her Jetta and drives Coastal Highway. She stops at an art show in Carlsbad. She sits in the sun; she watches the surfers coming in. *The California life* she thinks, believing she lives in the most beautiful place. She thinks too about a new destination this year – why not Hawaii? She thinks it's time to let her former life go. She orders Mexican food and a soda. She eats outdoors with the breeze blowing her hair. She sends a silent little prayer to Nate – tells him to tell Dillon hello. The days turn to nights and she learns that Kim did not make it. They died together in that car. Jolene finds the words to express her sadness, "If only I knew then I could have helped her." She tells Jodi and he listens intently. She attends the funeral. She cries the hardest at the viewing. Says another prayer over her casket and a *goodbye*. Then she walks away. She returns home. She is alone. Jodi is back to work. The days are uneventful so she books a newborn, books a wedding. Books anything that will ease her mind. Her soul. She wants to breathe in their happiness – and she does. She moves through the days with photo shoots and when she returns home they are all there – *surprise!* She hears as she enters the doors. She first sees Gwyneth and she moves toward them; they are holding balloons, a lighted cake and wearing party favors.

"Am I turning forty or four!" She jokes.

"Four!" Rick says followed by a wink.

"You all do too much!" She is amazed.

"Not enough," Jodi embraces her and she kisses him back.

"Thank you," Jolene says.

They pop a bottle of champagne. Jodi moves the party outside. He tells her he'll be back. In a large acreage behind her house she sees streams of colors – fireworks are in a display in the yard where the house was removed.

"He's going to get us all into trouble!" She covers her mouth, laughing.

The display lasts fifteen minutes when he comes out of the weeds and the bush. They clap. On that evening he is the hero.

"He's a catch," Gwyneth says.

"Thanks, Gwynn," she says.

"Anything for you, Jo." Her sister hugs her tight.

Jodi is in his glory; he gets to both surprise and amaze his woman. She is thrilled to have them there; thrilled to see her sister in California, show her the new home and even spend a day at the beach. They make use of the time they have together. They shop. They lay on the beach – the men surf. The girls build sand castles. Jodi and Jack are both not too bad on the board. Jack is skilled in riding horses but in his travels he has learned the water. They take a boat another day and jet skis the next. There is nothing that they do not want to do together. Jolene talks with Gwyneth about plans for a wedding. She wants a fall wedding; the colors of the leaves changing, she looks to her sister.

"You need to have your wedding at my house. I want you there."

"I do too … but perhaps it needs to be different this time."

"What are you comfortable with, Jo?"

"I think we'll do a small, private ceremony on the beach."

"It's whatever you want."

"I want the smell of your cider … but I just can't do the same wedding twice."

"And you shouldn't. Do you have a day planned?"

"I'm thinking around October. On the beach."

"Be sure to send me an invite."

"I will, Gwynn. Of course I will."

"Jack and Jodi get along well."

"They do. It's a shame we don't live closer."

"Maybe one day we'll change that."

"Perhaps."

Jack and Gwyneth stay for another day then they are taken to the airport. Jolene and Jodi see them off; they are with Anna and Clara who gives her hugs and kisses goodbye. Jolene captures their moments in photographs and a passerby snaps a photo of them all together. They smile warmly in one another's company. They wave them off and watch the plane depart.

"I guess we'll see them again in October."

"Why October?"

"Gwynn and I planned our wedding in October on the beach," she laughs.

"Were you going to let me in on this plan of yours?"

"Eventually," she says as he's kissing her.

They leave LAX and make their way to Jodi's condo so he can grab a clean uniform from the closet. Jolene touches upon another point...

"Are we moving in together before or after the wedding?" She asks.

"Well, I'd have to sell the condo. I own it. Or do you want to keep it as a second home? It is paid for."

"I never thought about keeping it. I had always assumed we'd live in my place."

"We can. I have no problem with it."

"It'll make the commuting a little easier."

"Then I'll start moving some stuff in and we'll talk more about selling or maybe just renting it out."

"Whatever you're comfortable with."

"Sounds good cupcake." He grins.

"All right then, my future husband."

"Touché my future wife."

And they embrace while crashing at his place for the night.

Chapter Six

Jodi shows up to her house out of uniform. She opens the door.

"What?" She smacks him across the shoulder.

"What did I do?"

"We were texting! You didn't tell me you were right at my door."

"Well I …

"Where is your uniform?"

"I…"

"Did you leave it at your place?"

"Yes…"

"But we just talked about you moving your stuff into my place."

"I'm sorry. Honestly, I apologize… I wasn't thinking. I just wanted to surprise you."

She leaves the door open for him to walk in. He closes the door behind him.

"How are you feeling?" He takes a seat beside her.

"I'm fine. Why do you ask?"

"Well, everything with Kim…"

"What brings that up?"

"I thought you might like to know how much she got?"

"No, I really didn't care to know honestly…"

"Sorry, I was just asking."

"Stop apologizing. Is there something wrong? You're acting different."

"No. Not at all. I'm the same…"

"That crystal was given to us by Dillon's mother."

"I see."

"I really didn't want to mention it."

"No, I mean, you don't have to. I just thought Kim tried her best to turn the table…"

"She did blame you … but we've already discussed this."

"You're right. We did."

"Thank you."

"Can I make you some lunch?"

Jolene eats her meal quietly. This side of Jodi is odd – overly apologetic and concerned when he's normally a man who's by the book. She finishes her meal and is taken aback when he doesn't offer help with the dishes; she wonders if he is feeling okay. When she asks if he wants to go out he only wants to stay in: has something happened? She doesn't pry though. She lets him relax on the couch while she takes up a magazine; the first issue of *Cruise Life* is out and she decides to share it with Jodi – he is part of the first issue. He skims over the magazine.

"Wow, look there ... Greg Mann and Alayna O'Connor..."

"Right, but Boyd now that she married Rick right?"

"Yes. You're right."

So far he seemed perfectly on point but should no longer be surprised by their appearance on the ship.

"Are you set for your next cruise?"

"I will do the articles before the cruise takes place."

"Okay." He doesn't look up from the magazine.

He goes into the bathroom and closes the door when she gets a text.

"Why are you texting me from the bathroom?" She hollers at him.

"I'm sorry ..."

"Do I want you to bring anything home?"

"I mean did you want me to bring anything home," he steps out of the bathroom... "I can go out and get it.... In fact, I'll be back." He kisses her cheek and rushes out the door. He returns home an hour later.

"You changed your clothes?"

"Yes, I stopped by the condo."

He takes a seat beside her on the sofa.

"Saw a place today … located in Montana … thought we should go sometime."

"Where is that?"

"Where is Montana?" He smiles.

"You know what I mean." She snickers.

"Lake McDonald."

"The jewels of Montana."

"You've been there?"

"I haven't. Saw it in a magazine."

"*Country Living?*"

"Something like that."

"When we visit your sister, I'd like to check it out sometime."

"I think we can do that." She rests her head upon his shoulder.

"I made some arrangements for the wedding … beach wedding, close family and friends, and in October when it's cooler."

"Why don't you tell me about your day?"

"You don't want to hear that stuff all the time."

"A few cases of domestic violence … shit you see on TV … writing reports … street violence. Nothing I want you to experience especially every day."

"Greg got hold of me today."

"Oh yeah, what does he have to say?"

"Was hoping we could meet up at the Italian place … over a few cocktails."

"When?"

"Tonight if you're interested."

"I'm okay with last minute decisions."

"Nothing wrong with last minute decisions."

"Nope. Nothing wrong with a little spontaneity."

They meet up at the famous *Rosalie Italiano* place and Gregory and Elaine are there first; they reserve a table for four. The dining area is finely lit by low lighting and classical music plays in the background. They chat briefly about the weather and order their cocktails. When their food is served the conversation changes.

"What's the news on that crazy brother of yours?" Gregory opens a sour topic, and Jodi's tone changes.

"I suppose no news is good news as any." Jodi swallows some water.

"What news?" Jolene is perplexed.

"What? She doesn't know?" Gregory guffaws and

Elaine taps his shoulder.

Jodi chews slowly.

"He killed his fourth grade teacher with a pencil to the neck."

Jolene nearly drops her fork.

"I haven't discussed it."

"Well now is a good time as any."

"I'm sorry, Jodi, I didn't know." Jolene tries to lighten the situation, "If you want to talk about it…"

"He was a minor then. He's locked up in juvenile detention. Well, was, then they moved him to a mental health institution."

"How's that mother of yours?"

"She's still in the psych ward."

Jolene can see how hard this is for Jodi. She places her hand on his, "I have an event coming up…"

"Oh, yeah?" His eyes lock with hers.

"A book signing at *The World of Books*. In two weeks, during the book and chocolate festival."

"That sounds like my kind of place," Elaine says, and Jolene writes down the address.

The festival takes place near the Gaslamp District of San Diego.

"Sorry for mentioning it brother," Gregory says, and clears his plate.

"It's no problem. Just broke the ice on the topic." Jodi waves for the server.

"Another cocktail?" The server asks.

"Another full round on me," Gregory says.

"Tell me about your book," Elaine inquires.

"The title is *Twist* … a thriller about ghosts who the main characters don't know are deceased."

"They're Zombies," Gregory chuckles.

"Kind of. They're not alive … they're the undead really and then there's a twist in the plot."

"Should I ask what the twist is or should I read the book first?"

"You should definitely read the book first," Gregory says.

"I don't want to give it away … if you like to read…"

"Oh, I do like to read," Elaine insists. "I'll be there to get a signed copy of your book."

After dining they head out to the beach; the weather is hot and dry as the first days of June bring out the heat. The women sit on the beach as the men surf. Elaine mentions how she wants to have her first baby; she is two years younger than Jolene and says they have been trying and will be moving on to their first round of IVF in the upcoming weeks. Jolene can relate as she has been able to get pregnant but hasn't carried to term. She tells Elaine about her miscarriages, the nineteen years she was married to Dillon, and how the car accident nearly killed them both. She chats briefly about her dreams and talks about meeting Jodi – how she never imagined starting over. Elaine listens intently; she has been dating Gregory since college and they lost touch briefly after graduation and re-kindled their relationship four years later. Their jobs took them in two different directions. Elaine studied psychology and became a child therapist, and Gregory studied architecture and design; he is now employed as an engineer and designs ships, buildings and residential housing depending on the job for that year. Jolene wants to interview him for the magazine to talk about Cruise Line architecture and how the vessels are designed for safety.

"Might sound like a boring topic to Vicky," Jolene says, "but I think I can sway her."

Elaine also discusses her love for real estate and how she got to design their first home. While Gregory got to design their home exterior and lay out, she got to design the interior and pick out décor. Jolene mentions how fun it must be to design a home to one's own personal interests. Elaine says Gregory would also do the interview and would see the article as a means to grow his business. *Gregory Mann Architecture and Design* was developed three years ago and the business is prospering. Elaine talks about her family who live in Arizona and how they adore Gregory for his good looks, charm and intellect. As Jolene notices Jodi wave to shore she realizes how he has saved her in a way. How much she feels fulfilled again.

She talks about her sister Gwyneth and her husband Jack in Montana, and her and Jodi's plans to wed in a small ceremony at the beach. She tells her about Vicky and the magazine some more and how she has picked up more work as a photographer. Elaine asks if she will be writing another book and Jolene chats about her memoir and stolen journals.

"Why would anyone want to steal your journals?" Elaine asks looking perplexed.

The men come in from the water.

"How's the water feel?" Elaine laughs.

"Well now if you would come into the water you would know how refreshing it feels."

"We are too busy talking our life history," Elaine says.

"Then don't let us interrupt you."

"Did you know Greg designs buildings?" Jolene asks Jodi.

"A designer?" Jodi says, "How'd you get into that?"

"Stumbled into it really. A buddy asked for my help getting his house together, I helped with design and found out I'm very good at it. And went back to college for engineering and design… the rest is history."

"That's how we lost touch and then found one another again," Elaine says.

"Elaine was studying for her master's in child

psychology ... and then fell in love with interior design so she helps me out."

"And the rest is history." She laughs again.

"Isn't that right, babe." He kisses her.

"Which means I get to interview you about designing large ships," Jolene says.

"You mean for the magazine?" He is right on point.

"Yes," she says and they schedule a date for an interview when she'll have her camera ready. Over the next few days she enjoys her time at home alone while Jodi works. She invites Vicky over and they spend time in the sun by the pool. She tells Vicky of her plans for an interview and she is responsive.

"The article will appeal to the male audience," she says, and Jolene agrees.

The Royal Blue her headline reads *Built for Stamina with the looks of Diamonds.*

The magazine has a full run and a circulation of thousands. Her interview with Gregory is done at their home that is beachfront and priced at ten million.

"I had no idea the extent of their wealth," Jolene tells Vicky on their next visit.

"He built a cruise ship!" Vicky reminds her and they both have a laugh.

"We should do another magazine and call it *Mansions*," Jolene says.

"Now there's an idea…," Vicky says, "and you're just the person to do it!"

"I don't think I want to deal with that much business."

"Then stick with the writing and the photography. You're good at both."

"And I enjoy the leisure of it."

"What did you do before Dillon passed?"

"I've always been a writer. I wrote a novel and several essays and short stories for anthologies."

"What did Dillon do?"

"Dillon was an attorney…"

"Oh yes, I'm sorry. I already knew that."

"That's a sign we're getting old."

"My mind is not as sharp as it was at twenty."

"No, and neither is mine."

Jolene produces the article and it has a full spread center fold. This issue, number two, has a substantial turn out with a large circulation that begins on the east coast and spreads through the west coast. The readers respond with feedback; the magazine is especially helpful with their decision to choose a cruise ship. Jolene responds to their inquiries and begins a blog; her articles go virtual, and she answers questions about dining, amenities and costs. Vicky hires on two more writers and an editor since the magazine is prospering. Gregory enjoys his face being front page and notices his inbox fills with inquiries after the article goes live.

Jolene and Jodi walk Cash. They stop at an art display in Carlsbad. They drive Coastal Highway. Jolene gets lost in his green eyes. They let a painter sketch their image. He draws Cash into the portrait.

"Our only baby," she says.

"But maybe that could change." He rubs her shoulder.

"Cash is a fine name," the painter says in a French accent.

"Thank you," Jolene says to the painter, and she smiles at Jodi who takes her by the hand. They end their day in the sunset as Jolene takes photographs.

They have *Cuisine of Mexico* for dinner and feel spent at home. When she awakens in the morning Jodi has left for work, and she gets his text.

Chapter Seven

Let's have lunch, the text says.

Where, she replies.

The Village, he responds.

An unusual place for Jodi, but she contends and they meet and dine indoors.

"We usually eat outdoors," she says, "why the change?"

"A headache," he says. He's not in uniform.

"What happened?"

"I went to the condo and changed. Couldn't handle the sun."

"Have you had a headache like this before?"

"Had them frequently as a kid."

Jodi orders a turkey club combo and a bottle of beer. He usually drinks draft so Jolene looks perplexed as he orders. She wonders if the fluctuations are caused by the demands of the job.

She chooses to stay quiet and orders a fresh Mediterranean salad. They dine primarily in silence.

"You've been going back to the condo quite often," she breaks the ice.

"It's just a way to enjoy the quiet," he says with mayonnaise on his lip. Jolene wipes it off.

"How's the sandwich?" She asks as he takes another bite.

"It's fabulous." She thinks she sees some of his personality coming back. Jolene mentions her book signing and explains she'll be away for part of the day tomorrow. She explains that she landed a signing at the local arts building before she has the book and chocolate festival to attend. The book signing at the local arts council is scheduled for noon – Jodi will be at work anyway. They eat in silence. Jolene senses a change in him. She's concerned. What doesn't feel right? Why is he seemingly distant? Typically Jodi is very hands on with her; she asks if anything has been bothering him to which he says there's nothing wrong – he just needed to get something to eat to kill the headache. At the end of lunch, he says he's going into the station to finish up paperwork on the riot that occurred in the next town. Jodi is a California State Trooper and the job this morning took him to Berkeley. Jolene is a little surprised but she doesn't ask much about the job and the stress he endures on a daily basis.

She's just there to lend an ear if he wishes to discuss his job duties. They finish up brunch and he says goodbye and that he'll be home later after finishing up the paperwork.

"Okay," she simply says, wondering if the job will have him distant when he returns.

As the day progresses she picks up her favorite writing

utensil and tries to imagine journaling again but she cannot get into the feel of it. She feels drained of emotional energy and thinking about Dillon adds to the stress. She turns to her blog instead and writes a sweet little article on the topic of photography. She gets a response from a few followers who wish to have her services at their wedding and reception, a birthday party and a newborn shoot. She quickly fills her schedule with the dates and times and records them in her monthly planner. Jodi gets home late and says he's ready to lie down. She joins him in the bed and although he had a long day he affectionately kisses her neck and as she turns to face him he initiates a night of passion. He feels warm and gentle and romantic. He removes her silky nightgown and they make sweet love into the evening. They talk afterwards about their wedding plans and she falls asleep on his shoulder and when she wakes in the morning he has gone off to work. He has been putting in extended hours that begin at six o'clock in the morning and he doesn't get off until after six o'clock in the evening. She is especially pleased that he still made time to tend to her. As she gets out of bed she feels exuberant and cheery. She loves him and perhaps the changes in his personality are just due to stress. She gets dressed for the day and heads out to the local arts council where she promotes her book *Twist*. She has a following from her blog, and lands some sales from those intersections. Then Jodi shows up. He's in uniform and looks a bit bewildered.

"Hello," she says and her smile is dazzling.

"Why didn't you tell me you have a signing today?" He says gently.

She is disgruntled. "What do you mean Jodi? I told you

81

yesterday during lunch."

"What?" He's a bit aggravated. "We didn't have lunch yesterday Jolene." He places his hands to his holster.

"Yes, we did." Her voice quivers. "At the Village."

"I was nowhere near here Jo …"

"You were in Berkeley."

"How did you know that?"

"Jodi, you told me that yesterday while we ate lunch at the Village. You had the turkey club."

"Jo, I hate turkey. You were with someone else."

Her jaw drops to the floor. "I was with you!" She is taken aback.

"Let me look into this and I'll get back to you." He leaves the same way he came in – flustered and confused. Jolene is now equally confused.

That evening he returns home early.

"Have you decided we had lunch together yesterday?" She is livid.

"Of course we did." He sniggers.

"Then what was your problem…"

"Those damn headaches. Messes with me." He puts both arms around her and kisses her but she does not kiss him back. She still feels confused.

"You want to …" he motions to the bedroom.

"Oh, give me a break Jodi," she breaks free of his arms.

He pulls her back into him. She doesn't like the aggression. She feels attacked. She makes her way to the bedroom and closes the door. She hears the front door slam. She enters the living room and he is gone. The week flies by and they see little of one another. Jodi has been working later than usual. She phones Gwyneth who doesn't know what to say.

"Maybe he's bipolar, Jo," she says. Jolene feels like crying.

"Maybe you're just now finding out … as you learn more…"

"I don't know," she says, "but he feels like two different people."

Gwyneth invites her over in case she needs a place to get away for a while. Jolene talks of her upcoming photo shoots and the festival and tells her sister she may visit in a few weeks. Gwyneth is happy to have her sister, and tells Jolene to call back when she decides she'll visit. As the days roll on Jolene finds herself at the chocolate and book festival. She sets up her vendor table on the corner of the street. It is hot and the streets are full of pedestrians. She gets a lot of coverage at her table. She sells books and chats about the writing process. She gives out free book markers and all goes as she hoped. When the day wanes to evening she packs up the few books she has left.

Jolene decides to consult Elaine since they've become friends. Elaine believes the psyche can endure mixed disturbances especially when there is a high level of stress, especially on a daily basis. She feels Jodi needs special attention in the moments he's feeling the most stress. If the personality conflict continues then perhaps he could make use of some medication. Jolene thanks Elaine to which she says she's there any time she is needed. Jolene returns home to a candle lit dinner in their dining area; she puts her arms around him.

"I'm here when I'm needed," she says, and he puts his arms around her waist and pulls her into him.

"How are you feeling today?"

"Better now that I'm with you." And he kisses her, "I can't wait to make you my wife."

"My husband ...," she smiles, and he serves cooked salmon, whole potatoes and carrots.

"This is wonderful." They spend the evening in one another's company until he crashes into her and snores lightly. She takes out her pen and begins ...

There was someone else in the house ...

Her mind tells her to write a thriller. *Twist* is doing so well she wants to write another novel. Jodi comes through the front door.

"I thought you were gone for the day," she takes a running leap into his arms.

"Whoa," he says, "is someone feeling a little frisky?"

"Do you want to come in and find out?"

"I decided to take the day off." Then, she receives a text...

Hey babe, I'll be at the station most of the day. I'll be late. Have to do some trainings.

Now she is alarmed.

She texts back: *Jodi can you come home?*

She is nervous. She decides to pry.

"Have you found out anything about my journals? My entire collection of jewelry?"

"Not a clue. Your only lead... well, she has died."

"You need Kim?"

"That would help."

"I wish she were here..."

And then the front door swings open.

"I had to respond to a call," Jodi says in full uniform.

"Oh... my... God..." Jolene is lost.

"That's my brother, Jo," Jodi says.

"You didn't tell me he's an identical twin," she begins to sob. Her mind is perplexed and flustered.

"How in the world did you get out?" Jodi asks.

"Everyone is going to know the truth," Clayton says, wearing civilian clothes.

"What truth?" Jodi steps forward, ready to break his neck.

"You're a liar ..." Clayton begins to break down, "you shit! You stole my identity. We were just kids you lying, worthless schmuck!"

"What the hell are you talking about?"

"You're not Jodi! I am! You lied after you killed her! Pretending to be me."

"Now you've really lost your mind, brother."

He turns to Jolene. "He's deceiving you!" Clayton says, "I'm the real Jodi."

Then he turns to Jodi, "I'm the real Jodi and then you took my name. Put me away and lied ... it's all lies..." He sobs.

Jodi remains calm.

Three dressed officers appear at their door.

"Hey Jodi," the older one says, "I hate to do this ... but we're here to take you in."

"What the hell for?"

"Sorry, boss," the younger one says.

"We'll explain at the station," the middle one adds.

"Being taken in for what?" Jolene can't stand the

suspense.

The oldest sighs, "The murder of Kim ..." he cannot complete his sentence when Jolene blurts out, "Kim was an accident!"

"Unfortunately there's a surveillance camera ..."

"Someone, they say is Jodi..." the youngest continues.

"An officer in uniform," the middle one adds... "Pulled the plug."

"Prematurely," the oldest finishes.

They ask Jodi to walk with them willingly. Which he does.

"You won't get away with this, brother," Jodi says. Jolene wants to throw herself onto him, but she resists.

"You must leave," she says to Clayton.

"I'll prove to you I am who I say I am," he says, and bypasses the officers out the door. Jodi goes with them voluntarily and at the station he is put in solitary confinement.

He contemplates how to show Jolene his true identity. Jolene phones Gwyneth, then Vicky and Elaine; Gregory cannot take the news. He's known Jodi for too long. Gwyneth invites Jolene to come stay with her and to stay calm. She has further obligations and cannot leave until the photo shoots are fulfilled; she has always been responsible. Vicky stops by after hearing the news. Jolene is consoled by her presence. She cries.

"I wasn't prepared for anything like this."

Vicky hands her a tissue. "Who would be?" She says, and Jolene wipes her tears.

"So who the hell is Jodi, and who is Clayton? Is that what I'm up against here?"

"Apparently, doll."

"What is there to do?"

"If I was you ... I'd hire a private investigator."

"I didn't think of that ..."

"Dillon was a hard core attorney... perhaps if you dig..."

"Yes, Adam Vanhaussen."

"So, you do know?"

"Yes, he was beside my husband in many cases."

Jolene digs into her husband's files that evening. She finds his stock of business cards and withdraws a card with Adam's name and logo. She pencils the number and goes to bed. After a long night of rough sleep she wakes up to shower and takes her card to the office and dials his number into the home phone. He answers after the third ring.

"Adam," she is speaking fast, "you worked with my husband Dillon Page..."

"Yes, Mrs. Page... I know your husband well."

"You were business partners."

"We were a good team, Mrs…"

"Call me Jolene."

"No problem, Jolene. Can I be of assistance to you?"

Jolene explains her situation. She talks of Jodi and his twin brother Clayton, and how Jodi has found himself in jail … an officer of the law behind bars. She talks of the alter personality she questioned, and how Clayton claims to be Jodi.

"A case of stolen identity," Adam says as he takes notes.

"Apparently." Jolene feels remorse.

"Well, they wouldn't have proven any differently through DNA," Adam explains, "because identical twins are born of the same embryo and have the same DNA." That much he knows. Adam takes on the case after gathering enough information. He schedules to see her in person. She leaves the appointment in her planner and leaves to see her first client; the newborn shoot is hard for her; Jodi's talks of children stay with her. Now he's in jail. She moves through the photo shoot quietly and with poise. She says she'll get through this by finding the truth; in her own mind she is furious; the pain is replaced by anger. Her confusion makes her question if she has been deceived. She thinks of the man she met and how uncertain she is now. Both sides of that personality revealed stress and commitment, and loyalty and brevity. They were not at any time a demeanor of a convicted felon – not that she could sense. They both retained a sense of humor. She thinks of the family Jodi told her about; if there is anyone who knows a son it would be his mother. She keeps that information in the back of her mind. Her first appointment with Adam is scheduled in a week. In that time she has a wedding to shoot and a birthday party the week after. She doesn't know how she'll get to the magazine articles but even though Vicky understands she doesn't want to let her down. She returns home after the outdoor shoot, confident she has exceptional shots of the couple's newborn. She sends her sister a text.

I'm anxious to find his mother, it says and her sister responds within the hour.

What do you already know, she sends.

She's here in California... an asylum I think.

Her sister takes some time to think before she responds.

That's a red flag.

Don't judge me ... the person I know isn't like that.

That you know of ...

Jolene is torn. She half resides with her sister – you never truly know a person – or do you?

Chapter Eight

Jolene meets with Adam. She is anxious.

"What do you have?" She asks as they shake hands.

"I'm going to begin with the basics," he says and she nods as she takes a seat.

"Okay." She speaks softly.

"Jodi McCain is currently being charged with first degree murder after a hospital video surveillance showed a fully dressed police officer enter her room and remove the breathing apparatus that alarmed the nurses, and they were unsuccessful at reviving the patient after the apparatus was removed then replaced, causing her to go into cardiac arrest. He's being charged with murder in the first degree of Kimberly Turner. Now, his brother Clayton, was charged with first degree murder of his teacher, Mrs. Martha Cohen, who was stabbed in the neck with a pencil when Clayton and Jodi had been kept after class for detention. Clayton was ultimately charged, Jodi was the key witness."

"But now Clayton contends he is Jodi and that Jodi has been lying… falsifying he is Jodi."

"I have more…"

"Okay…"

"Their mother, Marlena Kathy O'Neil, their father and she never wed, has been institutionalized since she was found under a bottle of whiskey, high on ketamine and declaring that the world was going to burn in hell for corrupting her only son Jodi."

"What about Clayton."

"Mrs. O' Neil says Jodi was corrupted by Clayton and her only son is Jodi."

"So she disowns Clayton as a fraud."

"She does."

"Do you know where she is located?"

"The asylum for the critically insane outside LA."

"Maybe she has a lucid understanding of Jodi's true nature."

"Perhaps. One could only hope that a mother knows her own son."

"Then maybe I should pay her a little visit."

"If she is lucid enough to speak. The critically insane can be heavily medicated."

"Making her normal."

"Just be careful."

"Do you have anything else?"

"That's what I have for now. If you need continuous help then reach out. Today is on me … you don't have to pay me. Your husband was a good man."

"And a great attorney." She smiles. "Thank you."

"Any time." He walks her to the door.

She enters the hall thinking of Marlena and hoping she can pay her a visit after the birthday party shoot she has up and coming. She goes home. She is restless. She dreams Jodi is home and she turns on the light. She considers making another entry into her journal but screams instead; she is alone, tired and sick of life going wrong and awry. She sits up and puts her feet over the bed when she sees her text: Clayton says ...

Can we talk?

She wants to respond *no I do not*, but her mind wonders.

Jolene instead texts back: W*hy*

And although it's two o'clock in the morning she receives a response: *So you can get to know the real Jodi.*

Jolene is not amused. She remembers the Village, wondering which Jodi likes a turkey club. She chuckles ... the other Jodi hates turkey – makes thanksgiving easier, she muses. She tosses her glass of ice water into the sink. It breaks and she huffs. Then she notices Cash wants outside and she opens the door. The night is still warm. The stars are abundant against a black sky. There are sounds of the beach; she grabs her camera and with Cash in tow she does some night photography. She thinks the birthday party will be grand too; it's an over-the-hill and a surprise for a husband turning sixty. They want photos for memories. Another potential client left a message: he wants a photographer for wedding proposal photos. She's booked. She decides to make him her last session for the month. In the night, she photographs the lights over San Diego; she names her file *Street life*. There are party goers leaving the bars. Many are unique and eccentric. She asks if she can photograph them. Many are drunk or on drugs but she doesn't care; the camera doesn't discriminate. They are pale, dressed in black and their hair is electric blue. She is happy among them – if only to be twenty-one again. She walks the streets as Cash sniffs the ground. She wishes they would be holding hands again. She thinks about the magazine; she thinks about Marlena; her mind is busy and the lack of sleep is taxing. She takes a photo of the bar at the beach; as he is closing she asks to take a photo. She'll capture anything she can to see the world through a lens that captivates the happiness of others. She returns home an hour later and returns to bed, and when she awakens from four hours of sleep she charges her battery and places her camera on the counter. She takes a shower and begins her day concentrating on meeting Marlena – destined for LA and she enjoys the ride despite the context. The day is a cloudless blue and the sun is vibrant. She feels exuberant, perhaps hopeful, in the heat. She lets down her hair, puts on a little makeup from her purse and finds the building where Marlena was known to be; she shuts off the engine and enters the front door. She is asked by the receptionist to sign in which she does.

"How may I help you?" A young, friendly front desk personnel asks.

"I'm here to see Marlena O'Neil."

The employee trifles through some pages and types onto the keyboard.

"You may have a seat in the visiting room." Jolene

has a seat, waiting for Marlena to arrive. As they bring her in she looks frazzled and grumpy. Her hair is wild and white. She has a doll at her chest and she clings to it. She wears a hospital gown and doesn't have teeth.

"Who the hell are you?" She is frank. Her demeanor is flat.

"I am Jodi's girlfriend ..." Jolene hesitates for a moment but she responds in the most honest way she can.

"Jodi never mentions a girlfriend..." she says, and snorts a little when she speaks.

"My name is Jolene."

"My son should have mentioned you."

"I'm sorry to come by like this ... it's just that we could use your help."

"What help?"

"Well, I was hoping there was a way to tell Jodi apart from his brother?"

"I only have one. Jodi is my son," she looks away.

"Can you tell me what is special or unique about him?"

"Jodi has a good soul. He's very smart."

"What does he do for work primarily?"

"Wouldn't his girlfriend already know that?"

"It's just … small talk."

"You'll have to ask him dear," she grunts to clear her throat.

"Well there's been some complications …"

"I haven't met Jodi's girlfriends since Connie." She huffs.

"Who is Connie?"

"A little girl he called his girlfriend. A sweet little neighborhood girl."

"He must have been very young."

"Just kids."

"He was teased by other boys in his youth because he liked a girl… those boys managed to strip off his shorts at a pool party. The kids got a good laugh. Jodi just turned around and stuck out his rear end… the girls got a good laugh, too. Jodi knew how to take control of a bad situation. That's when Connie noticed his birthmark." She chuckles almost pleasantly. Jolene thinks she sees her glow a bit.

"A birthmark?"

"Oh, yes. Under his ass on the back of his thigh. Looks like the state of Texas we joked."

"Connie saw this birthmark?"

"I'm sure they all saw it," she gets a little disgruntled.

"I'm sorry, this must be hard for you."

"Mrs. O' Neil," a nurse walks in, "it's time for your bath."

Jolene grabs her purse.

"I'll mention this when Jodi comes to visit." The nurse walks her out of the visiting room. Jolene is anxious. She didn't realize Jodi has a birthmark – but Jodi doesn't visit her either. Not her Jodi anyway. She returns home to take Cash out for a walk. She contemplates how to find out about this birthmark when she thinks of Alayna. They spent a decade together – surely she must know him well enough – but embarrassing enough that she isn't certain. She'll give anything to prove his identity and his innocence. On her walk, she passes by one of their favorite places to eat. *Cuisine of Mexico* is busy outdoors but she decides to stop and have something to eat while Cash lies beneath the shade. The daylight wanes to evening as the sun begins to set and her food is served. She has the chicken enchiladas and gives Cash some of the leftovers. She feels she needs to visit Jodi. She also has plans to visit her sister. She takes up her phone and decides to search Alayna Boyd and she finds many but Alayna's face is crystal clear. She sends her a message. She puts away her phone hoping Alayna will respond. She pays the bill thinking of Jodi when she decides she'll visit him this week before she intends to leave to visit Gwyneth. The summer is especially hot in June and next week will be July. Jolene decides she'll attend their cookout for the fourth. When she returns home she gives Cash a bowl of water. He laps at the water as she receives a response on messenger.

Hello, Alayna says, *great articles!* Jolene is happy she is being friendly.

Hi Alayna, Jolene responds, *thank you ...*

No problem. Do you need help with the next one?

No I'm sorry, I have a question about Jodi...

Ask away, I'll try to help.

Thank you. Did you notice a unique birthmark on the back of his thigh?

Omg, no, never. Jodi doesn't have any birthmarks.

Is it possible you may have overlooked it?

I don't think so. You know?

His mother tells me he has one...

You actually met her? She's crazy ...

She is elderly and well a bit disturbed...

No, she's completely nuts.

Okay, thank you.

Any time.

Great. She follows her text with *hugs*

Jolene enters the office. She takes a seat behind Dillon's massive oak desk. She cries. She's overwhelmed when she receives another text. This time it's from Clayton (or is it Jodi) which says: We *still need to talk.*

She doesn't respond. She turns her phone off. She gets a drink from the wine cabinet and wishes to see Gwyneth. After having her glass of wine she goes to bed and dreams of Jodi – the way he would touch her – the warmth of his lips against hers. She misses him. She awakens to Cash snoring at the foot of her bed. It is five o'clock in the morning, and she turns her phone on to find more texts and she deletes them. They go unread. She later phones Vicky who is at the gym; she texts back: *How are you?*

Hanging in there.

Jolene inquires if Vicky can watch over the house; she plans to take Cash but Vicky says it's no problem to watch him – anything for a friend. Jolene accepts her offer to opt to a hands free week with Gwyneth. Jolene flies in and they pick her up at the airport. When Jolene arrives at their luxurious cabin she unloads her bag in the guest room. They have thirty friends and family invited to the cookout. Jolene and Gwyneth's cousins are there; their children play on the large blow-up splash pad. The weather is warm with full sunshine. The Fourth of July is spent outdoors with a BBQ. Jack grills the chicken as he marinates the breasts with barbecue sauce and adds burgers and hotdogs. Jolene sips on wine along with her sister. The day is bright with some cloud coverage, and Jolene feels good in their presence. Anna and Clara play in the pool. Jolene and Gwyneth bask in the sun.

"You know," Gwyneth breaks the silence between them, "I know some pretty nice single guys who don't have all that weirdo drama attached to them."

"Dating is the last thing I want right now, Gwynn."

She sips from her almost empty glass.

"Need some more wine?" Gwyneth asks.

"I'll get some more here in a moment."

"I'm just trying to help."

"I know you are … things are just complicated right now."

"But it doesn't have to be."

"I guess not if I just give up on him."

Jack interrupts them, "What can I get for you ladies?"

They both take a hotdog and Jolene picks from the fruit platter. She is affected by the lack of regard from her sister and wishing Jodi could be there – wishing things could go back to normal between them – how much she wishes he didn't have a twin. She considers why Marlena only cares for Jodi, for only one of them, and certainly she must care more for the one who isn't evil. She wonders if there is a way to bring justice back to them no matter which is the golden child – she just wants the truth. Gwyneth tries to console her with opportunity, including meeting another man, but Jolene doesn't feel comfortable with the topic. Gwyneth changes the conversation to her own news: she is pregnant with baby number three, and it's a boy. Jolene is happy for her. She hugs her sister and the family joins the condolences. Gwyneth is shining and Jolene feels like falling apart, but she keeps it together for her sister. This is her day – and she is only trying to help. She wonders if leaving Jodi is an option. All she knows is that she wants him back. Her focus turns back to Adam – she wants his help in proving Jodi's innocence. She thinks about the full uniform – not knowing how Clayton could pull that off. She sobs. When she musters the nerve to call she is relieved when Adam picks up the phone.

"Adam, you're answering the phone."

"My secretary is out today. What can I help you with?"

"I got in touch with Marlena. I paid her a visit. She says that Jodi has a large birthmark on the back of his thigh … that's something identifiable."

"That's a start Jolene. Another identifier for twins are unique fingerprints."

"Is that something you can do?"

"I don't do it myself. This is where Jodi should be able to help you. Have you been to visit him?"

"No, I haven't. And Clayton has been trying to talk to me."

"See what you can find out especially if they had been fingerprinted in their youth."

"I'll see what I can do."

"They should have Clayton's prints from the incident he did as a child. They will match them up."

"What about stealing Jodi's identity to get away with the crime?"

"Then perhaps both were printed. Even at birth. Do some digging."

Jolene says "okay" and they hang up. She is not sure where to begin so she starts with calling the police station to find out visiting hours. The clerk instructs her on the hours he can have visitors which are Wednesday and Saturday nine to noon. She plans a visit for Saturday after ending the call. His prints should be within her home – but to match them with a print from birth – the best way to know for sure who is Jodi and who is Clayton. She keeps this information to herself and prepares to make her visit during the hours she was given.

Chapter Nine

The waiting line is long; they will begin to unlock the doors in ten minutes. Many who wait are smoking cigarettes. She brushes the smoke from her face. Once inside she moves through the metal detector and deposits her purse in the bin where they go through her belongings. They search her body and she gets moved to the waiting room. One at a time the inmates file through the door; when Jodi enters he is pale and his lips are chapped. They approach one another, take a seat and pick up the phone; they talk through glass.

"I saw your mother..." she says flatly. She doesn't want to give in to her emotions.

"My mother chose to defend Clayton, everything he's done, and she's defended him."

"She only recognizes Jodi as her son. She says that you visit her..."

"Clayton is stealing my identity Jo... he's taking my life ...," he rubs his hand over his closely shaved head. He tries to calm down.

"I'm left with having to prove this ... to prove that Clayton is not me. Not Jodi."

"The only thing that separates twins is fingerprints." She omits the birthmark.

"There are prints of us both in early childhood ... in books that are probably stored away and I don't know

103

where. Clayton and my mother have been locked up for some time."

She tells him about the private investigator, Adam Vanhaussen, who was acquainted with her husband. She tries to put a little faith in the man she knows. They speak briefly during the thirty minute visit, and Jolene leaves and tries to contact Adam. Once on the phone she tells Adam about the stolen belongings from her property and informs him of the report she filed. Adam says it doesn't look good – Kim stated Officer McCain came back to the party and went through the personal items. Then, the surveillance shows him visiting her hospital room and removing the tubes that supplied oxygen. He says he'll work with the police to get the area dusted for fingerprints and the paperwork will take some time. Jolene is concerned; only Jodi helped her in the moving process but the desk is likely full of prints from the moving company personally. Still, she's hopeful and she's keeping her fingers crossed. She plans to see Jodi on Saturdays and she'll accept his call in the evenings. She meets with Vicky to discuss the magazine; Vicky tells her to take some time off and that she has some freelance writers to fill in for the time being. She also tells Jolene that she has a fabulous attorney in the family and that she should give him a call; his name is Ned Warner. Jolene takes the information from Vicky over the phone and thanks her for all her help. Her next focus is on her text from Alayna, who says that Jodi does not have a birthmark – after a decade with the man she should know! Jolene is bewildered and frustrated. Now, she takes the call from Clayton. His voice is smooth, quiet and reassuring. She does not want to offend him – she only wants to get closer while keeping her distance.

"Hello," he says.

"You wanted to talk?" She says back casually.

"I need you to know I'm not what they said I am…"

Jolene listens carefully as he describes the traumatic day in detail:

We were kept after school for not being on task. My brother and I were always in trouble for talking while the teacher was talking. Her name was Mrs. Cohen and she didn't seem to like us much; she mentioned unruly children once. My brother made me a slingshot for my birthday and I once shot her in the back of the head with a marble. She had it out for me after that. She could not make us out at all; she never had our names right. We had to tell her who we were … that's when he did it. She asked him his name. He said he was Clayton and he took the pencil from her desk and that's when he did it. The paramedics were there. Then Clayton said he was me. He took my name and my identity. The real Clayton did all this. My brother is not Jodi; I am Jodi and I never struck my teacher with a pencil. The man you know as Jodi is Clayton and he killed Mrs. Cohen that day after school. He wiped his hands of it when he took my name. Then Jodi was innocent and became a cop while I was sent to the juvenile detention facility and was later transferred as an adult. I got some good time and got released. But now I am here to take my name back and my identity. Our mother has paid the price too … they said she was crazy … the only one who is insane is my brother Clayton. I am going to prove this …

She stops him there. "I am too," she says softly. "Can we meet tomorrow over lunch?

"Yes. Where?"

"The Village. Ten AM."

"One of my favorite places. I'll be there."

"I'll see you then." She ends the call.

She knows it'll be weeks before they begin the finger printing. She enters her office contemplating. How many prints will be on there? She thinks about her journals — who would take them and why? She has a restless night of sleep and gets out of the bed by seven o'clock in the morning. She brushes her teeth and showers. She pulls up her hair and applies makeup. She leaves the house at eight with Cash in tow. She can walk to The Village and they dine outdoors. The seating is sparse and it is quiet. Clayton takes a seat affront her and she says, "I'm sorry, but for now I must call you Clayton …"

He nods, "That's what I've been for a while now." His tone is subtle. His demeanor mimics his brother's. As of yet they are not greatly unalike. She wonders if Jodi has a personality imbalance as previously suspected. He is simply dressed in khaki shorts and an army green collared shirt. She feels as though she is with Jodi; she reminds herself that she is with someone who may or may not be a criminal — and that the cop she knew is facing charges. Her stomach turns. She feels sick. She orders a simple salad and enjoys a sweet tea with lemon. Clayton is smooth and orders the turkey club. Her mind races. The man she knows as Jodi dislikes turkey.

"I hope you understand I just want to take my life back," Clayton says and her mind whirls as she contemplates being with Clayton — a murderer and a fraud.

"No one would blame you," she is calm, "if what you

say is true."

"I wondered if you'd like to come by for a swim?"
She's contemplating the birthmark. She is eager, anxious,
and wants her life back, too. She waits briefly as he says
yes and when? She tells him that she can use the company
after they eat – later on that day. Evening will be good.
She excuses herself to the ladies' room and sends a text to
Vicky. Together they can invite some friends. Vicky
responds that she is free but feels anxious around
Clayton. Jolene understands but she explains that right
now he is simply trying to get his life back. Vicki
responds that she'll be over around eight o'clock in the
evening. They schedule to meet up and Vicky asks to
bring someone she met recently; his name is James
Godfrey, and Jolene says to bring him. She makes her
way back to her seat and tells Clayton they have a date
scheduled. He is anxious to meet Vicky. Jolene pays more
attention to her salad and hides her nerves. He talks about
the years he's missed. How ironic it is for a felon like his
brother to conceal his identity as a uniformed officer.
Jolene listens and eats slowly. Cash is panting under the
table. She feels better with his presence. Clayton primarily
eats in silence aside from when he is talking about the
years he has missed. Then he mentions his mother – how
she had a visitor. How he is close to her and how
"Clayton" was a menace to his mother. She cannot image
Jodi as this person – but how well do you know
someone? They finish their meal and she asks where he is
staying. He says he's got a little place not too far away,
but he is not specific. She says okay and tells him she'll
see him at eight. When she returns home she prepares
fruit and cocktails. She cleans the pool. She thinks about
Jodi and she cries. She loves him – the person she

believes to be him.

Back at the station those who know Jodi speak with him briefly. The police chief who he refers to as "boss" and the young cadet who refers to Jodi just the same, tell him they'll get him back in uniform. Jodi doesn't cling to the bars with the other inmates. He drinks water, swallows down the day's meal, and writes in a notebook.

"We'll do everything we can to get you out of the cell," Officer Chip says. Roy Chip has been police chief for quite some time. He leaves the station daily at noon during lunch to visit Jodi in his cell. Jodi doesn't say much. He doesn't know how Clayton would be in possession of a uniform – his own uniform. He wonders how long Clayton could have been following him – contemplating how to take his identity. Jodi sits behind his pen contemplating his innocence – his life as a uniformed officer – how he has never seen this coming. He writes in his notebook to best use his energy constructively. He goes outside and waits; he waits to go inside where he can be alone. He hears of the inmate who served thirty-seven years in prison until DNA freed him; he was wrongly accused. He considers how DNA cannot free him and he considers what he's up against.

Back at home, Jolene gathers the platters she has made and takes them beside the pool when the doorbell rings. She answers the door to find Clayton with a bouquet of yellow roses; he knows what she likes – or is it a coincidence? She takes them as he enters the door. She shows him outside and he compliments her on the nice aesthetic of the pool. Shortly after that Vicky and James ring the doorbell; Vicky wears a sun dress over a white two piece swimsuit.

"It's nice to meet you," James says. He is older, nearly fifty, dressed in a Hawaiian top and flip flops. She likes his swagger.

"It's so nice to meet you, too. Come on in."

She introduces Clayton as Clayton and the two men give a firm handshake. Jolene shows him to the restroom where he can change into his swimsuit when he says he forgot to bring one.

"Do you want to wear Jodi's?" She sighs.

"That'll be just fine." He doesn't appear uncomfortable.

She finds a navy blue pair Jodi would never wear and hands them to Clayton. He enters the bathroom. She doesn't hear the door lock. She waits by the door. She then grabs another pair from the drawer and she opens the bathroom door.

"I'm so sorry," she says, "I thought you may not fit those..." She throws the new red and black pair into the toilet; wearing briefs she cannot see well, but he bends over.

"Oh, what is that on your back... the back of your leg," she says.

"What?" He says, and she turns him around.

She gets on the floor to inspect his back.

"Is there something there?"

And she sees it. A large birthmark peering from his briefs

on the back of his leg. She grabs a towel and acts as though she is wiping his lower back.

"It looks like it was just a smear."

He blushes, "Ah, okay?"

She leaves him to change in the rest room and shuts the door. She remembers Marlena's words – her Jodi has the large birthmark on the back of his thigh. Clearly Clayton has a birthmark – a mother should know her own son. Alayna and she know Jodi doesn't have a birthmark. She makes her way outside. She shakes her head. Vicky reads her: "No?"

"According to his mother he's not Clayton. He's Jodi with a birthmark."

Vicky gasps. Jolene grows quiet. She hands her a glass filled with cocktail. She raises a toast, "to friends", and Vicky chimes back, "to friends." They drink. They swim. They dine on platters of pepperoni and cheese; they drink cocktails and talk into the night. When morning arrives Jolene takes his glass. She takes it to the station; she gives the glass to Chief Officer Roy Chip and he places it in the line of prints to run.

"I can get back to you as soon as I can." She thanks him.

She returns home to find Clayton still asleep on the sofa. Vicky and James are in the guest room. Jolene feels cramps in her abdomen; she takes a pain medication. She may have partied too hard. She tells Clayton she has errands and he leaves after requesting a drink; his head is spinning and he takes some pain meds. He drives a two door coupe; she thinks how it doesn't match Jodi's desire to drive a truck. The truck that sits in her driveway; she prefers that truck. She phones Adam and leaves a message; he returns her call quickly and she informs him she has a glass to compare prints. He informs her to keep the glass in plastic and to drop it off before business hours which she heartily does that day. She sees Adam briefly as he takes the glass and tells her he will touch base with the forensics personnel he is acquainted with. He asks for a good date to dust the desk, and she makes an appointment for the following week. She quickly exits the door and when she returns home she finds the house is empty. She wishes to call Kim and the thought sinks in – did Jodi kill Kim? What could he wish to cover up? She decides to soak in a hot bath to pass the time. When she is done she decides to check her phone messages that are from clients; four phone calls later she has the week booked with clients. She smoothes a brush through her hair and towel dries the ends. She gets a text from Gwyneth; she wants to visit her in California. She sends a text back: *Would love to have you.* Her response is sweet: *The four, I mean five, of us are anxious to visit!* Gwyneth wants maternity photos. She shares the news on Facebook now that she knows the sex. Jolene is happy for her younger sister. She is delighted to do her maternity phones. Jolene phones Gwyneth.

"Sis," she says upon answering, "don't you want photos in Montana?"

"Nope. We want to do it on vacation at the beach!"

The news is good news to Jolene, and Gwyneth and her family plan to fly in two days. Jolene learns her sister is 28 weeks.

"It's a boy," she says, "We've named him Henley."

Jolene is anxious to have a nephew. She hears from Vicky who believes she lost an earring at the house. Jolene keeps the forensics information to herself. Jolene has Vicky over and they look for the dangling opal earring but nothing turns up.

"What do you think about James?" She asks, glowing.

"He's a lot of fun."

"And good looking!" She protests.

"Of course!" Jolene snickers. "Only the handsome ones for you, Vic."

"That's right, Jo." And she changes the subject, "What have you found out about the imposter... what's the latest beyond the birthmark?"

"Just that so far ... the man I know as Jodi does not have a birthmark..."

"You also proved that through Alayna ..."

"Yes. And Clayton has a dark birthmark on the back of his thigh... who his mother says is Jodi."

"A mother should know."

"She's insane for a reason."

"But Jodi could be odd at times?"

"I think so. I'm not sure."

"This whole situation – how confusing for you!"

"It truly is."

"But do you think you could, you know, move on?"

"I've done that already – after losing Dillon."

"I know you have, love." Vicky gives her a warm hug and Jolene notices an earring staring at her from under the glass table.

"Oh, there it is!" Vicky says as Jolene scoops it up. "It was a gift from James."

Jolene and Vicky decide to have lunch off Coastal Highway. The weather is bright and the heat is in the nineties. They sit beneath an umbrella in the shade. Jolene tells Vicky of Gwyneth coming with her family – of her pregnancy. How happy she is for her sister. Vicky is happy for them too; she never had children. Her ex-husband worked too much. They never had the opportunity. Vicky wonders if she'll do an article for the magazine and Jolene speaks of the freelance shoots she's picked up, but in the matter of a few weeks she'll be ready. As they speak her phone chimes; Clayton is wondering if she can talk.

It'll be later this evening, she responds, and tucks her phone into her purse. At the moment, she is content and happy; she just wants to enjoy her girl time and chat. For this day, nothing feels wrong and she likes it that way. They order toasted sandwiches with lots of veggies and order a margarita. Vicky's smile is warm like Jolene thought of Jodi's. She misses him and wants to resolve this problem he's found himself in; they are in together. She wipes vinaigrette dressing from her lip and they watch as the surfers come in. She doesn't mention the fingerprinting she's having done because if she cannot locate baby prints she has a feeling it's going to spiral out of control in a spiraling motion making her mind whirl. She drinks from her margarita and contemplates – she has clients lined up until the room gets dusted. That'll keep her mind occupied a while. That, and Gwyneth coming in – tomorrow could not come soon enough.

Chapter Ten

Gwyneth and her family land at ten o'clock in the morning. Jolene is waiting for them, and as they leave the plane Anna and Clara go to her. She receives warm hugs and that feels good. Clara talks about graduating high school and the baby that's on the way.

"It'll be interesting starting all over again," Jack says, and Gwyneth is glowing.

"It's exciting for us to bring a baby into the family again."

They make their way to baggage claims and each one takes a suitcase. When they get to Jolene's, Adam is waiting for her.

"I'm sorry to surprise you here, Jolene, but I'm glad you're home. I can have the dusters here within ten minutes …"

Jolene is surprised. "Okay." She knows she'll have to explain to Gwyneth.

"Dusters?" Gwyneth is perplexed, "Like a maid?"

"No," Jolene is calm and reassuring. "They are looking for fingerprints."

Jolene opens the front door and they file inside. She offers them a beverage and some snacks. Clara and Anna are content on their electronic devices. Gwyneth looks concerned, but she is quiet.

"I wish better for you than this," she manages to whisper.

"I want to help Jodi," she says, "whichever one that may be."

"This is all a bit Hollywood, don't you think?"

"No, this is my real life," Jolene says with a sigh.

Jolene peeks through the door as she lets the surveillance team into the office. She observes their actions as they lightly dust and take photographs. They have some positive prints as Adam gives her the thumbs up; the process takes less than thirty minutes. The team cleans up their gear and heads back outside. They load their truck and Jolene watches them pull away.

"Running the prints for a positive match will take a few days," Adam explains, and she nods. He tells her to have a good day and he'll be in touch within the next couple days.

"Let's do something a little more positive," Jolene says and Gwyneth beams.

"Maternity photos," she claps.

"I'll grab my camera."

"Yay!"

Gwyneth changes clothes and looks chipper with a round belly in a plush dress that hangs off the shoulders. They go outside into the heat of the day. Jolene finds some palms and stages her between the two lush palms and some ground bearing plants. The session is three hours as

Jolene captures their moment in twenty-five outstanding images. She edits during their review and the shots are uploaded into a CD in digital prints they can develop when they return home. The remainder of the day they head to the beach; they have margaritas by the sand from a beachfront bar. The girls body board and Jack rides in the waves while the women have their social time. The day is bright in California and they discuss shopping and walking the boardwalk in Santa Monica. They head to the hills after their day at the beach is spent and Jolene ignores a call from Clayton. She cannot endure his pleads of conviction for his brother – who she knows as Jodi. She wonders if they did prints at the time of Mrs. Cohen's murder. She assumes they have and perhaps these prints will settle the matter quickly.

Before she can proceed to think anymore, Clayton is at her door; she peers through the peep hole and darts across the entrance to close the office door. When she returns he knocks again and she opens the door.

"Do you need any help?" Jack says, and she closes the door.

"No," she says firmly and ushers them to the outdoors.

"I don't know how to introduce myself," Clayton begins when interrupted…

"You just did. Have a seat I guess," Jack says in a short tone that mocks his impatience.

"Thank you," Clayton musters as if not getting the joke.

Gwyneth eyes Jack and he shakes his head.

"Cocktails?" Jolene asks, and they agree a drink would be nice.

"So we'll find out who you are when those prints come back," Gwyneth says and Jack disrupts. "I think all that is Jolene's business, Gwynn," he says and she looks away.

"It's no problem...," Clayton remains vigil.

"Oh, it's all definitely a problem," Jack says and Jolene returns outdoors.

She serves Bahama Mamas on the rocks and they sit together while the girls enter the pool. The silence is awkward. Clayton senses the tension. No one mentions the prints. Jolene is confident the prints will end the problems soon. She sips gingerly and watches the girls play. Jolene thinks about Jodi. About his innocence, or his keen ability at deception. She's left to wonder when it is over.

"I cannot stay and hold you up any longer," Clayton says and Jolene stands.

"I'll walk you out," she says.

When she returns, Gwyneth looks fierce. "You should not be talking to him, innocent or not."

"He's the only way I can prove Jodi's innocence."

Jolene thinks of the birthmark. She is frustrated.

"Gwynn here kinda let him in on the fingerprinting,"

Jack huffs and Gwyneth shrugs.

"Gwynn, you didn't?"

"I just want him to know you're not stupid."

"That's was for me to do, Gwynn. That's my business."

"That's what I said," Jack stands and kisses her on the head. She brushes him away but gently.

They spend the week together by the pool, on the beach and on the boardwalk. They do some shopping. Gwyneth has Clara to get ready for college. She gets some new clothes and a purse. Life feels normal. Jolene doesn't feel out of touch with reality as Gwyneth must think of her. Then reality comes in the form of a text: *I completely forgot,* she says, *I have someone I'd like for you to meet … his name is Jared.* Jolene thinks as she sinks in her chair. She pours a glass of wine. She considers a hot bath. She wants to soak in luxury then she receives a photo – and he is handsome: dark, straight white teeth, gleaming smile, sharp jaw-line, dark eyes, and sleek black hair.

Tell me how you know him, she writes back.

Jack met him at a convention – an old car show – and they chatted about convention – and introduced him to me. He's on my social media. Single.

Jolene laughs to herself. She thinks a man like that should not be single – so what's wrong?

Why is he single?

Gwyneth writes back, *Jo, his wife passed last year from cancer. I told him about you and Dillon. He wants to meet you.*

Jolene feels in awe of his situation – two people who know about loss.

Where does he live?

Gwyneth replies quickly, *well he travels a lot for business but has a house in Vegas.*

Oh? What does he do?

He's a builder, designer like an architect.

Jolene thinks again about that bath. *I'll talk with him but can't promise any more.*

She leaves her phone on the charger. She runs hot water in her soaker tub. She hears the phone chime and decides to soak and relax. She feels funny but ignores it. Perhaps a good friendship will come of it. She lights some candles. Turns on soft music. Replenishes her empty glass and sinks into the water when there is a knock on the door. She ignores it. She cannot handle anymore of Clayton at the moment. She prays he goes away. When the knocking stops she lets out a deep breath and focuses on the ambience of the situation.

When Jolene opens her eyes there is Jodi, or Clayton, standing before her.

"Jo," he says, "I'm out on bail."

Her eyes widen. She's startled and breathless.

"I don't know what to say ... Jodi..."

"You don't have to say anything … I know this situation has been hard on you."

"Yes, it has."

"We can take this one day at a time, and maybe get all this resolved quickly."

"I hope so."

"I have some money and clothes packed. I can stay at the condo until you feel comfortable…"

"Okay, just give me some time."

"I can do that. Anything for you, Jo."

"I appreciate that, Jodi." Her voice is somber.

Jodi leaves the bathroom and she hears the front door shut. She is thankful for that condo. She needs a moment to think. She has clients to tend to this week. She wants the drama to be over but she also yearns for the truth – is he not what he seems? What is the truth to the past? Then she wonders if she should be concerned – or can she move on? She leaves the bath to retrieve her phone. She finds a text from an unknown number.

Hello Jolene, this is Jared. Your sister tells me you'd like to chat. I'm looking forward to hearing back from you.

She puts her glass of wine on the table and is ready to write back when a message comes through.

Jolene, it's the real Jodi here… Clayton has lost his mind. They've let him out of jail. Now he's here and I have nowhere to go.

She doesn't know what to do – the emotions are boiling. She's confused and throws her hands into the air. Then another message comes in.

Jo, he's been staying at the condo.

She is floored. Frustrated. She grabs her camera and leaves her phone upon the table. She meets her client at the beach; she's doing engagement photos – a client that would lead to wedding and maternity photos. She enjoys making long term clients. She has the sun behind her; the ocean is behind them. The day is bright enough for crisp, clear photos. She feels the happiness return to her body. She lives vicariously through the happiness of others. Her own body gets sick and she throws up; the stress is getting to her. Her clients don't know it. She leaves the ladies' room with a smile. She snaps shots of the ring glinting from the light. There are multiple poses she takes and they leave a three hour session feeling fulfilled. They go back to Jolene's place and into the office; she doesn't want to touch anything but she has to edit twenty-five shots. She compiles the photos onto a USB they can print later. She's fulfilled for the rest of the day, and she returns to her phone; there are multiple messages and one of them stands out to her.

I'm in California if you'd like to meet for dinner.

She feels spent from the day but she considers it.

She honors a break from Jodi and Clayton, and texts: *Sure. The Tex Mex at six … I'll Google it.* He responds and she takes her time getting dressed. There is only one she knows of as it's a family owned restaurant close to the beach on South end of "The Five." She chooses to wear a yellow evening dress that is floral and not too flashy. She curls her hair. Brushes her teeth. Puts on makeup. With a little jewelry she is finished and ready; last minute plans ease her mind. She walks out the door; for the first time in months she sees Jodi's truck has left the driveway. She gets in her two door coupe and lets down the roof. Her convertible is perfect for a warm evening. She speeds off down the strip and finds herself in San Diego. She is early but gets a table and orders some wine. She is seated outdoors and watches as the sun moves across the horizon and casts shadows across the deck. A man approaches the table dressed in simple jeans and a black tee. He is charming to look at.

"Jolene?" The man asks, and she smiles back at him.

"Hi, Jared." He takes a seat.

She likes the bit of scruff on his chin; it shows an imperfection that is charming. He works hard - doesn't have the time even for a date, but she feels perhaps he has tried his best. He's given a good effort.

"Have you been here before?" Jolene asks and he looks a little surprised.

"I grew up on Spanish cuisine. My father's mother was Spanish. From Puerto Rico."

"Wonderful. Then you'll have no problem with the menu?"

"No. Not at all," he chuckles, "but to this particular restaurant I have not been."

"You're in for a good treat. The food here is very

good."

"Is there something you recommend?"

"I'm getting the tortilla bowl with grilled steak, and the fajitas are excellent."

"Then I'll order the dinner for two – the fajitas platter with shrimp, steak and chicken, and a pile of grilled vegetables. I'll just take home what I don't eat."

"You know, maybe we both should have that."

"Sounds good to me." He folds the menu.

Soft music plays from a band. Jolene orders a margarita and Jared orders a Corona with lime. He seems casual and is already pleasant to talk to, but her mind veers to Jodi. She thinks how much he would love the fajitas and Spanish rice. She thinks about Clayton; how the name makes her shutter. She thinks about Dillon, too.

"My sister tells me you are also widowed? You lost your wife last year?"

"I actually lost my wife two years ago."

"I am so sorry."

"I am, too. She also told me of your loss – your husband passed from a car crash?"

They are mindful of one another's feelings.

"He did." That is all she can say. She doesn't want to break in the middle of their dinner.

"Vivian had stage four breast cancer, and she just could not survive it."

"Dillon was behind the wheel. A young man made a left turn and our brakes locked up."

"Such a shame."

"It is."

They are served drinks and endless chips with salsa. The moon is hovering and the sun gets lower over the horizon. The seagulls are in clusters over the beach. There are surfers among the waves and the restaurant is bustling.

"What will you be doing after dinner this evening?" He asks, and they receive their food fresh from the oven.

"I'm not sure about this evening … I have a photo shoot in the morning."

"So you're a photographer?"

"I dabble and do some writing, too."

"Then you'll like the art exhibit in town."

"What kind of art?"

"There are photos, abstract art, paint on canvas – it's quite eclectic."

"Featuring multiple artists then."

"Oh, yes. Several. Pottery, too."

"Sounds like a good time."

"It's open for display 'til about ten o'clock."

"Then that means we have plenty of time."

"Oh, yeah. Plenty." He dabs sour cream into a tortilla and forks a shrimp.

He talks of business and how he started his company that he now co-owns with a partner. They work all over the west coast. His home is in Vegas but he is thinking about selling. He is not home long enough to enjoy it. He lives out of suitcases and hotel rooms. He draws and designs — that she likes. He tells her of his daughter Samantha, who is twelve, and lives with her mother in Colorado. He has her on the weekends when he can, but admits he doesn't see her enough. Jolene doesn't mention her miscarriages but speaks of having wanted children when she was with Dillon. Jared doesn't pry. They leave dinner in a good mood and they drive in his Lincoln to the art exhibit. There are artists discussing their art. She finds the photographer and his work is stunning and simple: many black and whites of still life, landscapes and humans of the world. There are colors of cultures across the world, famine and abundance.

"There's not a topic he doesn't cover," she says and they walk toward the canvases, portraits and styles reminiscent of Rembrandt. The darks contrast with the light in images that are both harrowing and subtle. Jolene finds that Jared is pleased to be away from work and in the company of an adult although he cares deeply for his daughter and speaks of her throughout the exhibits: how she dances in ballet slippers and strikes a softball like Babe slammed a home run.

"She sounds talented," Jolene says.

"Oh, she is," he agrees, "for only being twelve especially."

Jolene doesn't want the evening to end but she has an early shoot pending. He takes her back to her car and they part after saying good night; she will not kiss on the first night. She also still respects Jodi though his drama has her down. She wishes there was never a Clayton; she thinks too that her husband should still be alive and she would not be going through all this. She sinks into bed and has a dream of him.

Chapter Eleven

In the morning she cannot help but to reminisce about her dreams; how they walked together hand-in-hand in a meadow that was still wet with dew. She washes her face and charges her camera's battery. She forgot after a long evening. She wakes to a text from Jodi: *Just want to tell you good morning. I'm here if you need me.*

She wants to share her dreams with him when another message comes through: *Jolene, I had a great time last night.*

She feels the frustration return to her. She opens a drawer to her vanity and there is a photo of Dillon; she is overwhelmed. She thinks about her journeys: one for every month he's been gone. Her thought processes become interrupted; Adam calls, and she answers upon the first chime.

"Hello?"

"Are you sitting down?" He is calm. Still soothing.

"Yes," she lies.

"We have matching prints on file…"

"Okay…" she's holding her breath.

"They are a match for Jodi of the police precinct, Jolene."

"Then…"

"What does that mean to you?"

"Jodi helped me move. It makes sense. Are there any more prints?"

"None that match the files."

"You got a match for Jodi … I'll start with that."

"Very well. I'll let you know if more comes through."

"Thank you."

They hang up and Jolene takes a seat. All she has is a confirmation that Jodi lives in her house; but did he steal and fake his brother's identity? Then there is a knock on the door. She peers through the peep hole: is it Jodi or Clayton?

"Hello?" She asks casually.

"Jo, it's me. Jodi." She doesn't feel safe. She imagines a pencil to the jugular – that horrific scene of the blood flowing from Mrs. Cohen's neck. She doesn't know who is earnest and who deserves life in prison. She opens the door.

"I don't mean to startle you, Jo. Life felt better when I had you in my corner."

She thinks he's speaking like a component – not what she wanted to hear.

"Jodi, things are difficult right now." She musters a half smile.

"I know, Jo."

Jodi doesn't have a mark on him. She thinks of the

previous text… who was assaulted?

"Did you find Clayton?"

"Using my name in my condo."

"What did you do?"

"I admit. I hit him, Jo."

"That's probably not good to do right now."

"I sat behind bars for that lying …"

"I understand, Jodi…"

"It's hard, Jo."

"It is."

"What can I do?"

"Nothing I can think of right now."

"Let me know if anything changes."

"I will."

She closes the door behind him. Her mind is frazzled. She wants to relax but she meets her next clients for a newborn shoot. They had a boy. He's only a day old; she ponders why she couldn't carry to full term – she considers Dillon who stayed by her side – should she be doing the same with Jodi?

She finds a rocky patch in the sand. The scenery is good for family portraits; they are exposed to the sun so she is grateful the baby stays asleep. She moves them to her studio she put together to finish the session. Her studio is simple and she's proud to have it put together in the remodeled attic space. She stations newborns in a wrap consisting of the colors the family selected. The baby blue is soft against a white background. He becomes restless but is soothed when fed. Jaime and Jason are in their mid-thirties and have their first. For some reason they give her hope. She lives somewhat vicariously through them. She edits the photos as they choose the shots they want and she loads them onto a CD. She is grateful for a hobby. Vicky wants to meet soon for a girl's night out. This night is as good as any and she hopes Vicky is up for some spontaneity. She wraps up the session and her clients are pleased. They are beautiful. She turns off the lights and heads to her outdoor patio. She sends a short text and Vicky responds an hour later. She has nothing going on and wants to meet at the bar overlooking the beach. They head to Santa Monica where there is a bar on the beach. They dress in a wrap and tanks looking similar. Vicky is elegant in soft pink and Jolene dazzles in blue. Once they've ordered cocktails Jolene tells Vicky of her date.

"He sounds wonderful," she says, "why stay in another's drama anyway?"

"I'm not sure exactly and it's been stressful lately."

"Of course it is!" Vicky can't imagine being in her shoes.

"Would going on a cruise help your mind?"

"Not right now, Vic. I have clients lined up."

"What about writing for the magazine?"

"I haven't been writing lately."

"Anything on those journals of yours?"

"Nothing."

"That's a shame. I do hope they turn up. You know, maybe Jared is just what you need."

"Perhaps," she smiles to hide her unease.

After their meal, Jolene heads home. She vomits. Something isn't right. She feels off like her head is in a daze. She splashes water on her face and towel dries her face. She goes into the bedroom and lies upon her bed on her side. She drifts off until morning. When she wakes it is raining and she cannot do an outdoor wedding in the rain; she checks her phone and the bride-to-be has sent her a message; the wedding is postponed until the following Saturday – easy to do when the wedding is in the back yard of a lavish estate. Jolene is certain she wants the day to go perfectly – they have made arrangements around a million dollar wedding. Jolene now has a free day and wishes Gwyneth was closer. It doesn't take long into the morning when she receives another message: *Jolene, it's Jared … you up for some tennis or a walk on the beach?*

She is most definitely not up for tennis, but she feels she might handle the beach if the rain stops. *It's raining here,* she types, *where are you.*

He quickly responds that he's leaving a job site and could be there in an hour. When the hour goes by the rain has not let up; it's calling for a total wash out through the day. Jolene schedules to meet for lunch; she wants something light and easy. Her stomach is in knots. She heads north bound on The Five and stops at a little barista where they can have coffee and a sandwich. She is hopeful that the light meal will go easy on her stomach. Jared is perky as he arrives on a Hog. Jolene is laughing; he didn't seem like the Harley type. The rain had just quit and she thinks he must have had just enough time to take it out of the garage. As she takes a seat her phone chimes; that chime is Clayton. She ignores it. Jared meets her inside and they are seated at a table for two. Her stomach turns. Instead of coffee she gets tea and Jared orders the grilled turkey panini. She still settles for a sandwich – a vegetarian delight. She tells him of her cancellation and they chat about work. Then her phone chimes again. This time it's Jodi. She wants to answer the message. She excuses herself to the ladies room where she retrieves her phone from her purse. He simply informs her that there is a pending court date but not for another six months and he wants to see her. He invites her to his condo which she responds she must decline because she has other arrangements. She quickly types that she'll have room in her schedule for next week in between clients and she apologizes that her schedule is booked with photography clients. When her phone chimes she reads: *I'll always be here.* She departs from the ladies' room and returns to her seat to find that their food has been served.

"It cancelled the wedding but the sun is shining now." Jared smiles with a piece of lettuce on his lip. She laughs. Her stomach begins to loosen and she feels more relaxed. His demeanor is contagious; she wipes the cloth napkin across his bottom lip.

"I was saving that piece for later," he jokes, and she feels at ease. She wonders if she could feel this comfortable with Jodi again. A piece of her heart does miss him.

"The weather forecast said rain all day."

"Then God said for it to stop." He winks, and she sinks her teeth into a tomato, mozzarella and basil sandwich that has the perfect amount of pesto to go with it. With the clouds parting and the sun peering between clouds they finish lunch and head to the beach. They remove their shoes and put their toes in the wet sand. Jolene cannot get her mind off Jodi, but Jared offers a pleasant distraction. His thick chest and broad muscles are unyielding behind a tight tee and his heavy buckle on his jeans completes his look.

"How long have you had the Harley?" She enjoys their small talk.

"Been riding since the age of twenty-one," he says modestly, and she kicks up the sand with her bare toes. All is quiet in her heart and her mind. She tilts her face to the sun and takes a deep breath – a sigh of relief. Her stomach has settled. The beauty behind the orange sky relieves her anxiety. Her tension. Jared begins collecting sea shells. She joins him and they relish in the moment beneath the sun without the rain. She has forgotten her phone. Forgotten the weekly bookings of clients. She walks in the water; the coolness touches her ankles.

"We'll have to do this again sometime," he says, and she enjoys the streaks of gray hair that is blowing in the breeze. She tells him of her pending clients and the weekly schedule and tells him it may be a few weeks before she can get away. He's not demanding. He understands and has a busy schedule ensured for himself;

he'll be traveling to the north for a building contract. Traveling is how he met Gwyneth and Jack. They talk of Henley and the girls. Jared is fond of them; he says Jack is handy to have around. They laugh because he is handy and multi-talented. Jared says he admires them and Jolene feels comfortable in his presence. They walk the beach further and within the hour the rain is moving in among them. She says she needs to head home for some time to relax. She's picked up a client in the morning: high school graduation photos. He hugs her warmly.

"Let's not allow work to keep us too distant," he laughs, and she agrees. She heads home; there is an unfamiliar car in the driveway. She is cautious. She turns the door knob slowly and the door opens wide and she finds Jodi – Clayton – sitting in the living room. She's nervous but remains calm and casual.

"Jolene, it's me, sweetheart. I could not stay away from you."

"Jodi?"

"Yes …"

"Where's the truck?"

"I had to sell it … it took a lot to post bail."

"Okay …"

"Before you can say anything let me say that I could not stay away from you and I don't want to lose you … I thought we could help each other."

"Perhaps." Her voice is soft.

"I prayed for this."

"Okay."

She sets down her purse and her keys. She has a strange unsettling in her stomach. She keeps the interaction friendly and subtle. She gets a second wind; the rain outside her window is a torrential downpour. She fills a glass with his favorite, Jim Beam on the rocks, and hands it to him. He takes it casually and his eyes are like they are pleading. She settles for sparkling soda – her stomach muscles are intense and she doesn't want to get sick again. He says he is tired and she offers him the guest room. He says he'd like to chat a bit. She says she is tired too but needs to take it slow with all that is going on. She soon retires to her bedroom and he leaves for the guest room. Soon she can hear his faint snoring. She is pleased with the situation. She lies down in the bed and thinks her life could spiral out of control. She picks up a leather bound journal for the first time since they were stolen and she pencils: *There are times when I feel so completely off and not myself. I am out of focus and confused. It's a strange place to be and I think I need to calm the storm.* She chuckles as the storm out her window is raging with wind and rain. A lightning bolt makes her think of Jared on his Harley, then to Dillon before the accident – how calm the day was leading up to his death. How she could not see it coming. She thinks of his grave being saturated to eventually be dried by the sun. She has too much to think about. She doses off into the twilight zone when her mind dreams of life with Jodi; she is jarred from her sleep. She sits up in bed. It has been a long time since she's had a monthly cycle. She checks her watch: it is six o'clock in the morning. She has two hours before the photo shoot. She grabs an umbrella despite the rain has stopped. She leaves the house quietly. She turns on the engine to her car and leaves the house. She exits the garage and makes her way to the nearest grocery store where she buys a pregnancy test; she enters the ladies room. She does not wait. She uses the stick in her stream and places it atop the toilet paper dispenser while she pulls down her skirt; the results are immediate. Jolene is positive; she is pregnant. She begins to tear – she had no idea. She was so busy. She takes a deep breath. She is pregnant with Jodi's baby and she would have to break the news to her sister – forty and pregnant! She knows she cannot continue to see Jared; she needs to make this situation right. Something brought Jodi back to her at the time when she needs it most. She washes her hands and places the stick inside her purse. She exits and makes her way to the car. She contemplates how she'll break the news to Jodi. She picks up her phone and texts rapidly… *I'm pregnant!* She tells Vicky. It doesn't take long and Vicky responds: *What?!*

It is cute she thinks and texts quickly: *Yes!*

She goes home. She enters the door – he is still sleeping which she thinks is unusual for him but she thinks too that he couldn't have had much sleep in a jail cell. She shuts the door and places the test stick in a glass. She places it upon the table and she waits, then an hour later he emerges with an endearing smile.

"Sorry I slept so late," he says, and takes a seat at the table.

"Would you like a drink?" She pushes the glass across the table.

"What's this?" He is smooth.

"Take a look."

He removes the stick from the glass; the digital response is glaring.

"Pregnant?"

"That's what it says," she smiles.

"Is it mine?"

"Jodi…"

"I don't intend to be offensive …"

"No, I get it, and yes this baby is yours and mine."

"Then we have a lot to do." He snickers.

"Babies tend to require a lot," she agrees.

"I'm going to be a father."

But Jolene tells him of her miscarriages, and he listens intently and nods subtly. He walks to her and gets on one knee.

"You've already proposed," she laughs.

He places his arms around her and embraces her. He then stands and makes his way to the refrigerator and takes out the orange juice.

"I'm still thirsty," he laughs. He pours himself a glass and kisses her upon the cheek and makes his way to the bathroom.

"I'm going to shower," he says, and she moves from

the kitchen to her private en-suite and gets ready for work. She has Vicky to respond to, but she must get dressed for work. She turns up the music and feels safe – the stomach tension she felt has answers. And she is giddy. She always wanted a baby. And the song plays and she relaxes... Blissful.

Chapter Twelve

She is ten minutes early to the photo shoot. Her client Stacy arrives only minutes later. They are doing her photo op near an industrial park at the client's wishes. The condemned industrial plant offers plenty of background for engaging teen photos. Stacy is dressed in high waisted blue jeans and a tank. Her hair is long and curled. She had her braces removed a week prior. She has dark eyes and a dark complexion. Jolene takes photos by a tree, at the stairs with a brick wall for a background. She finds wild flowers growing from the nearby park and a deep blue sky above – the photo shoot cannot go any better she thinks. She feels that sensation in her stomach; she is eager to find out how far along she is in her pregnancy. Vicky has been blowing up her phone. After the shoot they wrap it up and she sends a quick message before starting her engine. She pulls away and meets her clients at the studio. They look at the digital images, edit those they wish to develop, and Jolene places the photos on a USB drive they can use to print as they choose. Stacy is sweet and she thanks her. Jolene thanks them too and walks them to the door; Stacy's mom is pleased with Jolene's professionalism. She checks her phone and Vicky has asked if she'd like to come over. Jolene responds: *How about meeting in the hills?* She cannot say why but she knows she just wants to window shop until she knows more about the baby.

Vicky exits her car and they walk Rodeo Drive and tour the shops of Beverly Hills. Jolene quietly wants a girl but she'd be perfectly happy with a healthy baby of either sex.

They browse the handbags, shoes and purses. Jolene buys one item – a tote. She wants to use it for all the things she'll buy if this pregnancy sees her through. Otherwise a tote has any good use really. Vicky walks out with a handbag for herself. They dine at a nice little Italian place and Jolene feels bad for the alcohol she was consuming.

"No wonder I couldn't carry … it's my life style," she says and Vicky stops her.

"No, it is not. Stop blaming yourself. You and Dillon had a great life together and it's not yours or his fault."

"I want this baby."

"I know you do."

"I have to tell my sister."

"Of course she'll be happy for you."

"She introduced me to a guy."

"What guy?"

"Jared."

"I guess he doesn't know."

"No, he does not."

"Has anything else been going on that I don't know about?"

"Jodi is back."

"The crooked cop?"

"Come on, Vic."

"Well, I know … but you know what I mean?"

"He's not crooked. He's just a cop who is being held under some pressure."

"Of course he is. I just hope he wasn't on the other end of that pencil."

"No. Definitely not."

"James is still visiting …," Vicky has a gleam in her eye.

"That's wonderful, Vic," Jolene says as she's served stuffed shells and a salad. The women eat gingerly, especially Jolene who is afraid of getting sick. She returns home after finishing her meal. Jodi is at home in the pool. He waves for her to get in. She walks outside and dips her toes in the water.

"Come on, woman," he says, ringing the ice in his glass.

She returns indoors and slips into a swimsuit. He turns up the music and she doesn't feel it should be a party. She asks about court and he shrugs.

"It's in six months," he says, and fills the glass from the outdoor bar.

"I'd offer you a drink but …"

"Yes, I know," she musters a laugh.

He enters the water and places his arm around her

shoulder. They look to one another and she sees the face of her baby's father. She is in awe in the moment. She shuts her eyes and lies upon a float. In the later part of the hour she retires to bed wondering if Jodi should still be occupying the guest room but it doesn't take long for her to fall asleep. In the morning she schedules a medical appointment, and come Saturday she begins a hectic schedule; she is booked with clients.

She has an outdoor wedding and this is her biggest project yet other than the magazine.

She stages her camera and begins photographing some of the arrangements; she places the wedding band on a twig emerging from the sand, wine glasses with the names of the bride and groom, and some of the immediate family alongside the guests. The bride asks her to capture everything and to not worry about money. They are wealthy. Jolene is honored to have been selected for the shoot. The bride enjoyed her portfolio and having done the cruise liner helped. Jolene is thankful for Vicky and feels she needs to do another shoot sometime for the magazine. The color scheme is classic black and white, and the place settings are fine china and crystal. The bride left nothing out of the décor. Jolene takes images of each party assigned to a table; the bride shall not be left without all the memories of her special day. Jolene thinks about her own plans for a wedding – pondering if she can resume a normal life – or is six months going to brutally change everything? She focuses on the wedding and when two hours is over she heads to the reception where the bride and groom are at the center of attention. She photographs their memories with thoughts of her own wedding with Dillon and how the autumn wedding in Montana had been the best day of her life. She leaves the reception feeling in awe of them and upon returning home she phones Gwyneth, not knowing what her reaction will be.

"Gwynn," Jolene says after she picks up on the first ring.

"Jo?"

"I'm calling to tell you some news."

"Jared spoke with Jack... says he's been seeing you."

"I'm afraid we won't be able to do that for a while."

"Why? What's wrong?"

"Nothing wrong ... I'm just pregnant."

"You're kidding ... by who?"

"It's Jodi's baby, Gwynn."

"Oh, no Jo, you're serious?"

"Yes I am. I have my first doctor appointment tomorrow."

"How far along are you?"

"I'm not exactly sure, Gwynn... I've been so busy I didn't even notice I hadn't had a monthly in quite some time."

"We're both going to have a baby!" Gwyneth chooses to be happy for them both.

"Yes..."

"How are you going to tell, Jared?"

"Nothing fancy. Just going to let him know."

They hang up the phone on good terms after discussing a bit about baby showers at Gwyneth's place. Jolene simply says she wants to take her time. Her pregnancies had never been successful. She's still nervous. The following morning she lets Jodi sleep. She attends the appointment alone. The office is not busy as she got a first morning appointment. She is let into the exam room. The medical doctor pulls up a chair.

"Do you know the date of your last menstrual?" The doctor asks.

"I don't," Jolene responds, "I'm not very regular."

"Well, we'll get you scheduled for an early sonogram and take it from there."

Jolene is thrilled and nervous at the same time.

"You want to lay back and we'll see if we can get a heartbeat?"

She does just that and the doctor listens to her stomach. A heartbeat is detected at one forty which is normal range, and Jolene lets out a sigh of relief.

"What was your weight prior to pregnancy? Any idea."

"I average one forty-five," Jolene says.

"Did you notice you've gained fifteen pounds?" The doctor is polite.

"Honestly, I hadn't noticed."

Jolene approaches the front desk and the receptionist schedules a sonogram. She is due back in four weeks at the office. The sonogram is scheduled for two weeks. Jolene leaves the building and starts the engine and rolls away feeling content at the moment. Upon returning home she finds Jodi lifting weights in the home gym. She thinks how the present drama with Clayton caused her to stop working out and she hadn't thought about it – perhaps that is the reason this baby is hanging on, and her and Dillon's haven't. She doesn't know, but she waits for Jodi to shower to deliver the news. He is earnest in his responses and she feels okay with the way things are, and she thinks there is hope for this baby. She explains she has a sonogram scheduled to indicate how far along she is in the pregnancy.

"By the way," he says, "I got a new number and a new phone. I'm going to send you the number now."

He explains how many jerks from the past are meddling into his business, and he hopes to refrain from more calls from friends who didn't turn out to be friends – they were just meddling.

"Okay," she says and doesn't think much else by it. She's preoccupied with the thought of the baby. She wonders if she's far enough to know the sex. She has a client photo shoot to attend to so she leaves home with her camera in tow; her client is a teen who will be graduating high school. She has many teens that want to be photographed in the summer just prior to their senior year – before and after photos are popular. It's the new in thing. She is taken to a state park; they are among the wild flowers, hiking trails, and a beautiful pond. The scene is very country, Jolene thinks, which is different from the typical California photos. They are far north. Jolene would like to capture nature photos of the red woods. She likes the idea of photos taken in the far Northern region of California and then inland at the end of the season – perhaps the teens are on to something especially for the opportunity for diversity. She thinks that Northern California would offer her own wedding the kind of balance she seeks between country and inter-coastal background. Jolene breathes in the fresh air and exhales. She feels happy in the lush greenery and she finishes her photo shoot by the pond where she is bitten by mosquitoes, and she laughs at herself for being so Californian she forgot her bug repellant. She thinks she needs a getaway once the clients are lessened but that doesn't seem to be any time soon especially with all the holidays coming. She packs her gear and heads south toward home but she doesn't think much about Clayton - it's as if she and Jodi can find peace among the chaos. As she speeds down the highway she notices Jodi's truck – unmistakable, not just by the tags but by the decals on the back window – decals that are unmistakable to his personality. She knows how hard it is to part with that truck. She heads indoors once home and finds Jodi asleep on the sofa, but he is easily startled by the closing of the door.

"I just saw your truck heading in my direction on the highway..."

He isn't startled as he yawns, "Sold it to Sam. An old

buddy of mine."

"Oh, okay," she says and tosses her keys into her purse.

"Have you been to the condo?" She's making small talk.

"Would like to sell that, too," he says nonchalantly.

"What are you doing for money?"

"I have a nest egg, pensions, retirement…"

"You plan to return to work?"

"Let's get through court. And have a baby."

"I mean before the baby…," she's frustrated and concerned.

"I can only do this one day at a time."

She gets it but still disagrees. She wonders why he is selling off his old life and she thinks he needs to re-think his strategy. His brother is making a grave claim against him and she hopes his nonchalance won't let him down. She's willing to fight – hoping Adam can deliver more news that sways the verdict.

She has three more clients, and then finds herself on Friday morning making her way to the medical appointment with Jodi in the passenger seat. They do this thing together, as he puts it. They are inside for fifteen minutes before being called back to the room. Jodi takes a seat on the chair and Jolene takes the examining table. They are seen by an ultrasound technician after the nurse checks her blood pressure, which turns out normal. The technician steps inside and warm jelly is applied to her abdomen. Jolene watches as the baby forms on the screen. There is movement and a heart rate sound. The tech takes measurements and pauses to print some of the exam.

"Are you ready for the sex?" The tech asks.

"You can tell that already?" Jolene is taken aback.

"You are eighteen weeks and four days along in your pregnancy."

Jolene turns to Jodi and he shrugs, and then nods.

"Go ahead," he says, and the tech turns to a view of the legs and Jolene can see she is having a baby boy. She is thankful, and she sends a telepathic thank you to Dillon who she sees as her angel. She feels blessed. When the session ends she is guided to a towel to wipe her abdomen as Doctor Griffith will see her next. They wait merely five minutes, and he enters.

"Everything looks good so far with weight and measurements. The only thing I can tell you is nothing in the vagina…"

"What?" She turns to Jodi. He is equally perplexed.

"You have a low level placenta that is right above the cervix. We will bring you back in eight weeks and do another observation."

"What's this mean for the baby?"

"The placenta should be more toward the uterus but yours is lying above the cervix, and the baby cannot pass through the placenta during birth and if that does not change you would need to have a cesarean instead."

"And nothing in the vagina ….," Jodi ponders.

"That's right. No douche, sex, tampons, stuff like that."

"Okay…," Jolene begins.

"Anything that could puncture the placenta could cause pre-term label."

"Ah." Jodi gets it.

They go home. They relax. Jolene thinks of her alcohol consumption when she hadn't known she was pregnant thankful it didn't go any further and thankful the baby is doing well. She thinks too of the hot tub – pregnant women are not allowed that kind of temperature so she settles for a hot bath. She touches her stomach – those flutters are now so well known. She has soft somber music playing in the background. She lights a candle. She hears the front door shut assuming Jodi is off to somewhere. Her phone chimes and she thinks twice about reading it but the curiosity gets the best of her: it is Jared.

Hello, he says, *I just want to congratulate you on your pregnancy. Jack passed the news.*

She responds in a good mood. *Thank you.* It is all she can say.

She thinks she and Jodi can get through this together – she hopes. In the back of her mind is Clayton's assertion that Jodi killed them … she becomes wary. Clayton must be a liar. A fake. She takes a deep breath. No one will ever sympathize with him so she decides to be a bit more covert and keep most of the pending goings-on between them.

She texts her sister: *It's a boy.*

Gwyneth is prompt: *How exciting!*

She places the phone on the hand towel and closes her eyes – she'll talk more later. She thinks for a moment – where is Jodi going? He could have said he was leaving. She huffs. *Oh well,* she thinks. As the candles permeate the room with lavender she drifts into a reverie of her and Dillon's wedding surrounded by the fall foliage, and she is excited for fall when she visits Jack and Gwynn and the girls. She is excited for her sister's soon-to-be new arrival and is happy they are pregnant together in this chapter that is new and exciting.

She sends one more text: *Have fun doing whatever you're doing.* She's a bit irritated with him, until she shrugs it off and dims the lights.

Chapter Thirteen

He comes home intoxicated. He is unnoticed by Jolene who is in bed. He scurries from the kitchen and into the guest room. He slowly shuts the door and collapses into the bed. He snores. She dreams of wildflowers and meadows. By morning she is in the kitchen making breakfast. He is asleep. It is Saturday. He awakens to the aroma. He vomits. She makes him a plate.

"Are you okay?"

"Must have been the seafood." He holds his stomach.

"Karaoke at the bar at the beach ... you're pregnant so I didn't want to disturb you."

"Okay?"

"I just needed to get out a bit ..."

"Right."

"What's for breakfast?" He pours himself an orange juice.

"What's on your plate?" She's edgy.

"Whoa, momma, snappy." He drinks from the glass.

She goes into the outdoors with her robe on. She takes off the soft cloth wearing a swimsuit. She is not showing. She dives in slowly and the water is a rush – a sensation like an aquatic massage. She thinks about doing yoga later.

Maybe Pilates. She wonders who Sam is – Jodi had never mentioned him and to sell his beloved truck sounds desperate. She hopes the trial is favorable – they need to see his lawyer – he hasn't mentioned that either. Maybe the nonchalance is comforting or a bit naïve. She floats on her back with her face to the sun. She is happy in that moment when it's just her and the baby. She contemplates his name. Jodi likely has his own ideas, too. She closes her eyes and shields her face from the sun; she cannot help but to think of Dillon – where has the time gone? The hour passes by and she returns indoors.

"I'm surprised you didn't join me." Her voice is soft, elegant.

"I didn't want to bother you." He rubs her shoulder. When Dillon would touch her she would get chills like an electric feeling. She is not sure with Jodi. She smiles and feels his smile is also genuine; he has glaring white teeth. She goes to her room to shower and is startled by a message on her phone.

Going to the Village Square. Want to join us?

She assumes Vicky means James will be going. She nudges Jodi who is on the couch.

"I'm fine with that," he says and takes her hand; he kisses it, "I'll get dressed." They get ready for lunch – the Village Square serves the best brick oven pizza and more. Jolene hasn't done much with Cash and when she returns she plans an evening walk with her furry friend. For now she and Jodi climb into her car and they take off for the beachfront tiki bar. They are seated and Vicky, along with James, follows after. Together they are a beautiful couple

Jolene thinks, and James shakes hands with Jodi.

"So you have some legal trouble?" James breaks the ice.

"Ah, well I do …," Jodi is thrown off by his forward nature.

"You mean his brother does don't you?" Vicky tries to lessen the tension.

"My brother is most certainly in some trouble," Jodi agreed.

Vicky and James order a mixed beverage while Jodi orders a beer. Jolene is happy to order a sweet tea and then orders an ice water with extra lemon to avoid the sugar. They order a light lunch: Vicky a salad and Jolene a light fish with mixed greens. Jodi orders a burger and fries while James gets the Cajun chicken.

"When are you due?" Vicky changes the subject.

"November 5th," Jolene smiles as she is served a tea and water.

"Have you thought of a name?" James decides to be easy on Jodi.

"Jodi Junior?" Vicky laughs.

"No, maybe Madison," Jodi says.

"Madison?" Jolene questions.

"My great grandfather …," Jodi says and his mood changes.

154

"Who?" Jolene wants details.

"My mother's father."

"How is Marlena?"

"When have you met my mother?" He is defensive.

"Jodi, you know I went to visit your mother."

"Yes, of course, I mean since she's had the dementia?"

"No."

Vicky looks to James and they eat quietly as their meal is served. Vicky has chatted about the birthmark. They say nothing. Jolene considers Marlena and what she told her; Jodi has the birthmark. Now she wonders if the dementia has been there all along.

"When was your mother diagnosed with dementia?"

"It's been progressing for quite some time."

Jolene feels as though she has found herself back at the beginning. She takes slow deliberate bites and her eyes meet Vicky's; they are on the same page and think alike. James smoothly and casually inquires, "Does she recognize you? My own grandmother didn't recognize us anymore."

"No, she doesn't. I visit but she doesn't know who I am."

"It's hard to go through."

Candace Meredith

"Yes, it is."

"I'm sorry she's gotten ill," Jolene says, and he appears flustered.

"Yeah," he says and excuses himself from the table and makes his way toward the men's room.

"We don't mean to pry," Vicky tells her, "we just want you to be safe."

"Thank you, Vic. That is thoughtful of you."

When Jodi returns to the table he finishes his meal in silence. They casually chat about the magazine; Vicky would like for Jolene to accompany her on another cruise. Vicky tells her the magazine has a broader circulation and Jolene is happy for her. She assures Vicky that she would like to be on another cruise. When they ask Jodi he simply responds "sure," and orders another beer. Their double date is virtually uneventful but Jolene likes the company and even if they are wary of Jodi she has Cash to return home to.

She enters the door and Jodi quietly goes into the guest room and shuts the door. There was tension among the men and Jolene feels he can sleep it off. She grabs Cash's leash and they leave the house to walk the neighborhood. The weather is still hot and very bright. As she rounds the corner she hears a car that has its brakes applied. The red convertible approaches her and she immediately recognizes Gregory and Elaine inside.

"Hey, how is Jodi holding up?" Gregory calls, and Jolene approaches the car.

156

"He got a new number, I'll have to give it to you and he's staying very quiet. Pretty low key."

"I cannot blame him," Gregory says and Elaine flashes her a wide smile. "That brother he has is really messing things up for him."

"Yes, and Jodi speaks very little about Clayton and the trial."

She informs him that the trial is set for six months out, and in five months her son is due.

"Congratulations," they tell her.

"Thank you," Jolene responds.

"I'm happy for Jodi," Gregory says, "I hope it all works out for him."

Jolene finally realizes that Jodi is pending a trial for first degree murder – for "pulling the plug" on Kim's life support and she doesn't know, really, if he pulled the pencil from Mrs. Cohen's neck – she was found covered in blood, Jodi said, and he was the only witness then, against Clayton – but did Jodi use his brother's identity: *Who killed her? Who killed Kim?* It's an epiphany for Jolene – their life is not normal and she understands Vicky and Gwynn's trepidation. The more she thinks, the less she feels she knows.

She gives Gregory Jodi's number and he programs it into his phone. Gregory says they'll need to meet up sometime for a double date or perhaps the next cruise. The rest of her walk is spent thinking, contemplating and pondering what she can do to help Jodi. She wonders if Alayna was dating Jodi or Clayton if Jodi had, all along, been lying about his birth name. *Birth name,* she thinks, she needs photos, anything, from the day of birth, to know firmly that Jodi has always been innocent – that Clayton killed his teacher. It weighs on her mind – an officer in uniform was seen in Kim's room. She gets chills. Is a monster living in her house? She phones Adam; she tells him everything in a fifteen minute phone conversation. He tells her he'll look into it and assures her he's there to help her feel more comfortable. She thinks mostly about the baby – she wants a for sure father figure in his life. The confusion makes her wary and she hopes Adam can deliver some news to ease her mind. For now she has Cash and the beauty of the weather all around her. She feels she wants to know Sam, to know Jodi's friends, to get an idea of himself through his own company. She finishes walking Cash in silence. Her California neighborhood is peaceful and she doesn't have to think about anything else momentarily. She likes the name Madison but something feels quite strange, and she thinks the name Hudson is more befitting and she likes the nickname Hans for a boy. So Henley and Hans ring a bell for her. When she returns home she takes out her calendar and begins to plan a trip to Montana and a cruise for Vicky. She has more photo shoots pending especially for newborns – and now she can begin to plan for her own photo op – but she's not getting too hopeful. It's still early in the pregnancy.

Her cell phone chimes. This time she is receiving a call - it's Adam.

"Hello?"

"Jolene?"

She is hoping for good news.

"Jolene, I'm getting back to you to let you know we do have two substantially different fingerprints. We have fingerprints from the glass you gave us and from the desk in your home; what we need are early prints such as when they were born."

Hoping their deranged mother could tell them apart during infancy, she thinks but feels badly about it.

"I'm not sure how to do that ... his mother is in the psychiatric ward living with dementia."

"It's our best solution ... but we can also push for a lie detector test but the results are not permissible in court in California."

"Jodi is with me ... I think a polygraph is a good idea."

She does not hesitate. She wants the truth and feels he should be out to prove himself, too.

"I can get in touch with the police department. They'll get something set up."

"Thank you," Jolene says

"No problem," he says, and they end the call.

Jolene feels it's her best opportunity to get to the truth. She walks Cash around the neighborhood once more – it is getting hot. She wants to swim in the ocean to get cool but she returns home and the pool is inviting once again. Jodi is in the pool already – Jolene laughs – he is wearing a Speedo. She dresses herself in a swimsuit and goes out beneath the warmth of the sun. Cash breathes heavy in the shade of the palm tree. She makes her way into the water. It's just the two of them again. He wades in the water and she asks him to get her a cold drink.

"No problem," he says and finds the stairs beneath the water. He emerges and she follows behind to stand in the shallow. The sun is glaring. She takes a deep breath – he has a birthmark clearly on the back of his thigh. She never once noticed if Jodi had a birthmark. She never needed to know. To look for it. If only their mother was a good, reliable source. Then as if reading her mind, he says to her, "We need to visit my mother." Jolene is startled.

"Sure. When?"

"Hoping later today. She needs an executive of the estate to look over her possessions."

"She has an estate?"

"A house and a storage shed left to her by my father."

"Where is the house?"

"San Bernardino."

"Okay."

"It's in rough shape but I can sell it to a flipper."

"Someone who flips houses?"

"Exactly."

"How late are visiting hours?"

"She's been put in hospice. They want me there today."

"Oh, all right, I can be there, too."

Jolene feels confused but hopeful that she merely overlooked a birthmark that is otherwise fairly hidden. She splashes in the water as she paddles toward the deep end and swims back; she used to want to be an Olympian Swimmer but she was in dance classes more often than swimming. She learned ballet and tap. She misses her mother. She misses Dillon; her life lately has been strange; she wants the truth and feels the loss of her mother all over again – the loneliness and the separation from them hurts.

Hours into the day Marlena sits upright on her bed staring out the window at a picturesque blue sky. She stares blankly.

"You a nurse?" She says to Jolene.

"No, ma'am…," Jolene speaks softly.

"Hey, Ma," Jodi says, and she looks at him quizzically.

"Who are you?" She says with her eyes slit.

"It's Jodi, Ma," he says and his voice is shaking.

Jolene understands the union must be difficult.

"I need a nurse," she says casually, "my pants are wet."

"You have a catheter, Ma, you should not be wet." He smiles at his mother but she turns her head.

"It's time for my bath," she changes focus.

"I just want you to know that I have everything taken care of." He pats her withered hand.

"Nurse!" She shouts with no attention on Jodi or Jolene.

Jodi informs Jolene that Marlena has passed three days later from pneumonia. She does not have a funeral but is cremated as per her early wishes she expressed in her will. She left the estate and her possessions to Jodi. Her urn is delivered home and Jolene places it upon the mantle where she thinks her old crystal would be located. She doesn't have much of an opportunity to meet Jodi's family because like her own they are primarily deceased. She is happy to have had a relationship with both her parents and was fortunate they never divorced.

Gwyneth texts Jolene asking if it's too early for a baby shower – they settle on having a shower in two months when Jolene is officially six months along in her pregnancy. She is looking forward to spending August in Montana where she can begin to enjoy the cooler weather and the changing season – something she misses in California. She intends to go alone without Jodi but isn't quite sure or confident – it's a baby shower intended for women she could tell him. She returns home with Jodi and they decide to enter the pool. She decides to bring up a conversation to feel him out.

"Jodi, have you ever known you have a large birthmark?"

He laughs, "Yes, since birth of course. I've been told it looks like the state of Texas."

She grins, "Yes, it does."

The flesh is darker in relation to his overall skin tone and in the Speedo he would easily tan and the birthmark would not be so visible. She's feeling angst over a birthmark. All she can do is shrug it off and pray or hope that Jodi can settle the score with Clayton in a civil way through court and then let the truth be known. She floats on her back in the water and stares at the blue sky.

"I like the name Hudson," she says, and he pours a mix drink from the bar.

"Hudson Madison it is," he says without argument.

"Hudson Madison McCain," she whispers to herself and pats her stomach that is growing more pronounced, and in the next few weeks she can feel the flutters knowing he's going to be okay.

Chapter Fourteen

Jolene begins her day taking engagement photos. They are at the beach in Santa Monica. The air is warm and the day isn't so hot – seventy-something in the shade. It's an off day for California weather in August. She's due to visit her sister and family next week. She spent the last two weeks doing photo shoots for clients who have new babies. She is enjoying life. She packs her bags and Jodi asks where she is going.

"I'm visiting Gwynn," she says.

"For how long?"

"For a week or two - I'm not sure yet."

"What will you be doing while there?"

"She is throwing us a shower."

"I guess I'm not coming along?"

"No, sorry, the trip is just for us women."

He nods and doesn't argue.

"Can you watch Cash?"

"I'm here to hold down the fort."

He can be charming.

She boards the plane and he waves her off. She has gone on a two week hiatus from work. From life. She goes to

Gwynn's to focus on the baby. Through social media Jolene is friends with Gwynn's friends. Gwyneth has a surprise for Jolene – Vicky has also made a flight to Montana. Gwyneth figured Jolene would like to see her there.

Gwyneth's home is beautiful like a getaway lodge by the ski resort. Jolene feels cozy there. They pick her up from the airport; Jolene is surprised to find Vicky waiting there for her along with the girls. Clara has not left for college; she will be a student at the start of fall. Anna will be going back to high school and will miss Clara; they are close.

"Not having her here will be hard," Anna says at the dinner table.

"You'll be the one to see Henley though," Clara says trying to comfort her.

"We are happier to have you here alone," Gwyneth says to Jolene.

"I am too. For now."

"For now?"

"I still hope for the best from a difficult situation."

"Isn't it, you know, scary that he could have done that," Anna says.

"Yeah, like he could have killed someone," Clara adds.

"Girls," Gwyneth tries to quiet them.

"It's okay," Jolene says, "I'm just trying to help him

prove his innocence." She forces a smile and Vicky chimes in.

"And we're here for you, Jo." She says.

"I know you are," she says, "I would feel the same in your shoes."

"Any of you girls want a cup of coffee?" Jack says from the kitchen.

"I'll take a cup since you're offering," Jolene opts for some caffeine as a replacement for alcohol.

"Maybe we can go out tomorrow for a virgin Pina Colada," Gwyneth says and Jolene looks happy.

"I'll take a virgin anything right about now." She laughs.

Jolene settles in the guest room and Vicky snuggles into the pull-out sofa bed. It is midnight in Montana and has an evening temperature of fifty-two. The high for tomorrow is seventy-four and Jolene loves wearing jeans. The night wanes to early dawn and the sun rising behind the mountains has Jolene outside on the front porch with a camera; the sun rising in the east is the most beautiful sky she has seen. She thinks about doing an art show at the local gallery with her photography – something to add to the list. She is momentarily interrupted by her phone and she retrieves it from indoors; there is a message from Clayton's number.

Jo, this is Jodi, the real Jodi, I need to talk with you.

She does not respond. She doesn't even talk about it –

she wants no parts of it. She turns her sound off and returns outdoors to capture the magnificent sun that rises above the mountains and shines an orange hue over the valley between them. She takes a deep breath and closes her eyes; she tries to feel with her heart and to let her gut instincts do the talking. She returns indoors and after getting dressed she heads downstairs to find in the kitchen a delicious breakfast, and Jolene wants to taste nothing but her breakfast.

Hours into the day it turns one o'clock in the afternoon and the women stop in for a dual baby shower – they are only a month apart in their pregnancies. They have a seat upon the sofa as the gifts are given to each one of them; no one is left out. The place is decorated with blue décor and accents on the cake with booties, pacifiers and ribbon. The day could not go any better.

"Aunt Margaret tried to come," Gwyneth says, "but her health isn't good for traveling."

"That's my mother's sister," Jolene explains to Vicky.

"Too bad she can't be here," Vicky says, "it's nice when you can see family."

Jolene enjoys the clothes, bibs and bottles she has received from the women – women who only know her through social media but they support her just the same. She puts the wipes and the wipes warmer and bottle drying rack back into the bags and thanks them all. When she gets to Vicky's gift she finds a lavish bag she recognizes from the day they went shopping; Vicky saw how much Jolene admired the bag and she got the last one they had left.

"I got it for you…," she says with a gleam in her eyes.

"Thank you," Jolene says softly.

"Anything for you," Vicky hugs her.

"It's so great to have all of you," Jolene gets tears in her eyes.

"We are blessed to have you too, sister," Gwyneth throws up her hands for a great big bear hug. The moment between them is intense. Genuine.

That's the answer I needed, Jolene thinks, *Jodi should feel like this … this is like feeling loved.*

She is pleased with her answer like being from divine intuition. Gwynn asks Jolene if she'll do the maternity photo shoot and Jolene feels blessed to have Gwynn; she asks for some photos to be taken as well, and Gwynn says she'll do her best. Montana offers lush green foliage and the weather is a mild seventy-four degrees. Heading outside Jolene takes her camera; she does a photo op of the shower first and once the guests leave they have time for individual attention. Although the photos are stunning, Gwyneth wonders if Jolene can come back next month or in October to do a fall theme photo shoot; Jolene is all for it. The fall season is Gwyneth's favorite time of year, especially in Montana. They talk passionately through the week about giving birth a month apart in October and November. They share their ideas of how to decorate the nursery – something Jolene hadn't considered yet. Their baby names are similar and they think the cousins will be close despite the distance between them. Jolene then invites them to attend a cruise together that is coming up for the Labor Day holiday; Jolene has promised to do an article for the magazine and will be attending the Royal Caribbean tour that lasts for a week. Gwyneth and Jack are interested and have the money and feel there should be no problem going on a cruise. They will simply bring Anna, but Clara will be off to college.

"My due date is around Clara's birthday," Gwynn says.

"You're due on the fifteenth?"

"The sixteenth."

"How does Clara feel about that?"

"She thinks it would be fabulous."

They toast over virgin daiquiris and enjoy the company of having one another and such great friends. Vicky boards a plane ride home and Jolene stays for three more days. She takes Clara to college along with her sister and Jack; Anna cries in the back seat. Clara assures her that when she begins her sophomore year she won't think about it so much and then she gives her sister an exuberant hug. Clara takes her luggage with the help of her family to the dorm room and is excited to begin her journey in college in Eugene, Oregon.

Jolene arrives home feeling exhausted and jet lagged, or maybe it's just the pregnancy, but whatever the case she feels drained. She gets beneath her sheets and dozes into an oblivion where only REM sleep can serve her well. Several hours later Jodi awakens her.

"How was your trip?" He nudges her shoulder.

She realizes they didn't talk much during her stay in Montana.

"It was good," she says, and he surprises her with a cup of coffee and breakfast in bed.

"Thank you," she says.

"Clayton tried talking to me," she has a slip of the tongue.

"Did he?" Jodi looks unnerved.

She sips from her coffee, "But I wasn't taking any calls." Then she changes the subject.

"We all would like to go on a cruise together next month," she says, and takes a bite of a warm hot cake.

"Who all is that?"

"You and I, Vicky and James, and then my sister and Jack."

"Sounds like a good time."

He appears casual. She isn't thinking of his pending court date; she's just immersed on living a normal life. Her life returns to normal the following day when she has a three month old photo shoot with a baby girl named Sophie. This shoot is done inside her home in her studio. Sophie is all smiles as she lies on soft, plush colored blankets and is photographed. Jolene is natural in making her laugh and the giggles are heartwarming. Sophie's mom changes her outfits but maintains the soft, plush palette consisting of pink, white and gray. Jolene thinks she'll have the best time with her own son as she sees their interactions. She has a medical appointment pending right before the cruise and she couldn't feel any more anxious – she loves to hear his heart rate on the doppler. Sophie continues to coo and laugh and Jolene's own bump is starting to show. Her nausea has dimmed down and she can eat a little better aside from the chronic heartburn she had the previous night. She's looking forward to October when Gwyneth has the baby and they can share such an experience together. She hopes Clara can visit too but knowing she's in college they may have to wait for the Christmas break – and then Jolene feels excited for that too. Mom and dad pose with their little Sophie and Jolene is all smiles with them. They are a warm and natural couple to be around and Jolene could not feel any more pleased and content. They ask her how long she's done photography and she admits she's relatively new; she speaks briefly about Dillon and how her hobby fulfilled her after suffering the loss of her husband. Jolene has multiple shoots planned including a returning couple and she's very excited for the opportunity to build her clientele. One such couple is Vanessa and Dan who are ready to have their maternity shots – after Jolene did their wedding they were thrilled to have her do more photos of their blessings. When the day ends Vicky sets up a time to meet to take Jolene shopping primarily for maternity clothes. Jolene's day couldn't get any better. They find a small café where they dine on ice water and salad with garlic bread. The weather is a fair seventy-eight and they sit beneath an umbrella at an outdoor table over-looking the pacific.

"Are you ready?" Vicky asks, and Jolene is confused.

"Ready for what?"

"Our next cruise," she says happily.

"Oh, yes, of course I am." She laughs.

"I was hoping you'd make this one. It's a fully booked liner and the guests range a good bit. Lots of diversity to write about."

"What kind of diversity?"

"The entertainment for one thing is different… there's jazz but there's also some cover bands who will be taking requests so the audience is quite diverse. There's a good bit of machines added to the casinos and the very large balcony where the pool is located along with an outdoor bar and so much to do."

"I'll be sure to photograph and write the latest."

"The magazine is doing well but it needs one of your columns or a full spread," she winks.

"Center fold is no problem," she assures her, "I got this."

"Perfect!"

"I'm looking forward to it."

They enter a few more shops after finishing their meal and Jolene finds dresses and some fall slacks to add to her attire for the ensuing weeks. She has gained ten pounds and she wonders how much more she'll be putting on. They wrap things up for the evening and Jolene heads home. She doesn't see Jodi and wonders where he may be but she decides to take a warm bath. During her soak, she views her phone to find another text but from an unknown number.

Jo, it's Jodi ... please respond.

But she cannot. She's too stressed with anymore of the debacle that may present itself if she answered. Certainly Jodi would handle his own brother if he could and especially in her place. She hears the front door slam shut and doesn't budge from her hot bath. She has jets that are loud so she couldn't hear him if she tried. The bath water turns cold and an hour into her soak she throws on a robe and enters outside where Jodi sits by the pool looking disgruntled.

"What is it?"

"It's me," he says, "It's my life and I must prove my innocence."

"Did something happen?"

"No, but I've been appointed an attorney."

"A public defender?"

"Exactly."

"It's hard to afford one I'm sure."

"It is..." His voice trails off. "Maybe some of your pension will help."

"My pension?" She says, bewildered. "That pension is from my deceased husband."

She is not amused and heads inside. She thinks to herself if she has ever mentioned anything of her finances with him. She feels she is a very private person especially when it comes to money. The only space she speaks freely is, or was, in her home office. She thinks about her journals – how much she wants to write again. *Did Jodi ever read my journals?* She feels confused. Her mind is too busy to sleep and she gets a glass of almond milk and a snack. She is bothered by this fiasco all over again – now what to do?

As the days move on he seems content and normal. She knows as a police officer he was not as endowed as her husband had been but she doesn't feel right using his money – or should she? She wrestles with the thoughts in her mind and keeps a cool composure while he is in her home. Their home. Is she stuck? She doesn't feel stuck at all but she feels confident lately and proposes they pack their bags for the trip. He does just that and assures her he didn't mean to offend her.

"I'm sorry," he says folding a tee-shirt, "I don't mean to step on any toes."

She believes he is merely anxious and the cruise may relax him a bit while she gets to work.

"Are we okay?" He looks sincere.

"Yes." She says.

For now, she thinks.

They put their hygiene products into another bag and he zips a duffle bag. They are set to leave for the cruise in the passing of the next few days. Jolene always did love packing early and he's just as secured following her lead.

He's at her mercy in a way, but Jodi knows the law and he will proceed to let justice do its duty. He not only has to prove his own innocence but Clayton's guilt. There is a great deal on their plate and Jolene will help the father of her baby – together they can get through this fiasco and be a happy and healthy family. Then Jodi finds his face in the paper: *California State trooper looking at years in prison.*

Jolene does not read on. The ordeal is spreading like wild fire and she knows he is growing more anxious. She takes a deep breath and asks for help from the other side – a prayer to Dillon to help her find her way, and all she can think is the cruise will be good for them. For whatever reason.

Chapter Fifteen

They leave port aboard the cruise liner from California to Mexico where they will visit Cabo San Lucas. Vicky meets Jolene in the casino where they can also dine for the evening. Gwyneth and Jack find their table and Jolene introduces them. Gwyneth looks radiant with a round abdomen and she shines. Jolene can feel her energy and embraces her sister. They are happy in one another's company. Vicky stands to her feet, waving, and Jolene takes a look –

"Gregory and Elaine, over here!"

"There you all are!" Elaine says cheerily.

"I had to invite them along," Vicky explains, "Jodi, how's it going man?"

Jodi stands and Gregory throws an arm around him.

"It's going," Jodi says, laughing with them.

"Do you two know each other?" James looks lost.

"Old college buddies," Gregory gleams, and they have a seat at the table.

"My little surprise," Vicky winks.

They order their first round of drinks when the liner leaves port. Jolene has a frosty glass of iced water with extra lemon. Vicky orders a mimosa cocktail while the men order pitchers of draft beer and Elaine is served a peach mojito. Gwyneth has an iced raspberry tea and makes the most of being pregnant. They order a platter of seafood including lobster and crab.

"Where is Anna during this trip?" Jolene is inquisitive.

"With Denise. Jack's mother."

"Of course," Jolene says, "that makes sense."

"Jodi," Vicky speaks smoothly, "does Gregory also know Sam?" She smiles.

"Who is Sam?" Gregory asks.

"Nah, Sam is a childhood friend. College buddies don't know him."

"He bought Jodi's truck," Vicky continues.

Jolene looks perplexed, but as they are served their appetizers they eat and chalk up other conversations.

"Hey Jodi," Gregory boasts, "I did see Derek the other day."

"Oh, yeah? What's he doin'?"

"Side jobs mostly. Never did get in with the DOD like he wanted."

"Well, why not?"

"Life." Gregory laughs. "Didn't have time for a Masters. Had a kid on the way and ended work."

"What kind of work?"

"Masonry a bit, and a lot of building. He's head foreman so doing pretty good for himself."

"That's great. And if you need some work until this whole thing blows over then I'm sure he can help you out."

"Well sure, I'll keep that in mind."

"I wonder if Alayna and Rick will have an appearance," Jolene flashes a glance at Jodi who is not paying attention but is eating.

"He owned the freaking ship last time right?"

"Yes, Jolene featured them in the article," Vicky says and asks the server for another round of drinks.

"So how are you doing with this whole Clayton thing?" Gregory looks concerned.

"I don't talk to him and I'm keeping my distance."

"That's probably for the best."

"Agreed." Jodi nods.

"You know you have other buddies to consider … I'm saying you didn't have to sell the truck."

"The money was nice."

"Does this Sam know Johnny?"

"Uh, no, I don't think they do … know one another."

"I see." Gregory is casual.

"Who wants to move this party to the dance floor?" Vicky asks.

They take care of the bill and head outside where there is live entertainment. The evening is picturesque; the sun is low and casts an orange presence.

"You can't get better than this view," a woman's voice says.

Jolene turns around to find Alayna and Rick.

"Best view I've ever seen," Jolene agrees.

"Alayna," Gregory says, "tell Jodi here about Johnny…"

"What is there to tell?" She laughs, "Nothing he doesn't know."

"He was a great character," Gregory winks.

"Right," Alayna says, "he truly was."

"Has Johnny passed away?" Jolene is lost.

"Jodi will tell you about him," Gregory says.

"Are you familiar with this Johnny?" Rick asks.

"It's a hard one to talk about," Alayna says.

"Jodi here tried to help him," Gregory says and changes the subject.

"Care to dance?"

"Love to." Elaine takes him by the hand.

"You?" Jolene says.

"Uh, I really don't dance," Jodi hesitates.

"Well that's too bad," Jolene says, "this will be your first." She cuffs her arm around his elbow and leads him out to the floor.

Jolene is looking for that feeling – for that connection. Instead he's awkward and clumsy. She doesn't hold it against him. The embrace between them is mediocre, she thinks. Perhaps he's just nervous; there is a lot pending for him. When the song ends they gather together and talk to Rick about Cabo … he recommends some of the best places to visit during their stay. They have an overnight visit at a grand hotel and a restaurant off the beach that serves the best seafood. Jolene looks pleased and there is no interaction between Alayna and Jodi; they have both surely moved on. When they port in Cabo, Jolene takes out her camera. She photographs the cruise liner and those she asks if she can photograph. No one turns her down. She includes Cabo in the article she intends to write – this cruise is a top favorite among the guests and she feels it should be a featured article. They retire to a hotel suite for only one night; the cruise will leave again the following evening. This cruise is a four day trip that is more affordable and she thinks that's valuable information for anyone who has not experienced a cruise will like to know.

She wonders about Johnny and poses the question that evening.

"What makes Johnny stand out from the rest?"

"He's an old drinking buddy," Jodi says, "from

college."

"Oh," Jolene says as he departs from the room.

"I'm taking a shower," he says and shuts the door.

Jolene exits her room with the intention to find Vicky, but instead she finds Gregory. He looks shaken but casual at the same time.

"Are you feeling anxious?" She asks in the hallway of the hotel.

"There's no way to say this …," he pauses momentarily. "But that's not Jodi."

Her jaw drops.

"Don't be alarmed or panic," he continues, "Vicky invited us because she was concerned… she thought we could help, but Alayna and Jodi can tell you the most about Johnny, and that's not Jodi."

Jolene is crushed. Deceived? Manipulated? She now thinks she does not want to return to that room. But she has no choice.

"I'm sorry to tell you like this." Gregory looks earnest.

"No," she says, "thank you for letting me know."

She is calm too. She takes out her phone and locates Jodi's old number. She sends a text: *Hello*, and waits for a response. She makes her way to an open bar and orders a raspberry sweet tea.

She receives a response: *Hello.* She takes a deep breath.

Can you tell me about Johnny?

There is a pause when he responds.

Who has told you anything about him so far?

She sighs. *No one. I need you to tell me.*

There is a long pause and she receives the message: *Come see me Jo, and I'll tell you all that I know.*

She is not happy but simply responds *okay.* She returns to her room and finds Jodi on the bed asleep. She decides to shower and sleep in the room with the sofa. The following morning she decides to pry, "What else can you tell me about Johnny?"

"He's just an old college buddy. You can conceive of the rest... just think fraternity."

"Okay," she responds and they exit the room. They enter the dining hall where they are to have breakfast and Gwyneth and Jack join them. They are served hot cakes, eggs, bacon and grits – a pleasantly southern dish. They laugh and joke together. Jolene feels abashed and dreads thinking she is with Clayton – her morose expression isn't giving her away. They don't notice. She eats her eggs without speaking. In five hours they will board the cruise ship and make their way back to California. Jolene expresses that she would like to experience the culture. Around noon they head to the beach. Jodi takes her by the hand - he's never done that before (not since he's come back home) and she wonders if he really does know Johnny. There's no electricity between them and his hand is in fact clammy, but she decides to do her best to hide her suspicions – Greg's suspicions.

At the beach Jolene snaps shots of each couple. Gwyneth takes the camera and returns the favor. Jodi brings shots from the tiki bar. He hands Jolene a raspberry tea – her favorite beverage while pregnant. Alayna and Rick join them at the bar. They order a round for everyone.

"Must be nice to be that filthy rich," Jodi says under his breath. Jolene slits her eyes in his direction so he grows quiet. The tiki bar is full and the guests get served beverages on the beach. Jolene interviews Rick again for the magazine.

"What is the best amenity on the ship?" She asks, and Rick is prompt.

"We have something for everyone," he says, "we have the casino, fine dining, the open bar, massive pool, live bands and dancing and so much more…"

"Thank you, Rick," she says when Alayna eventually pulls her to the side.

"It's hard to tell you this … but Jodi harbors a secret about Johnny… they go way back … but he will find it very hard to talk about it." She is sincere.

"Thank you," Jolene says, "he tells me they're just drinking buddies from college."

"No, he's not correct about that." Alayna is now serious, "We think he's deceiving you. Jodi knows that he's not a drinking friend and they did not attend college together."

Jodi approaches and asks what they are talking about.

"Just work," Jolene says, "the magazine."

"You have enough material for a column?"

"Yes, I believe so." She is concerned. She feels her stomach. She thinks she'll be sick. She excuses herself to the café where she can use the rest room. She begins to cry. She takes her phone out of her purse.

What is the secret regarding Johnny? She needs an answer.

You must be around Alayna.

Yes ....

She knows what I know .... It's a long story ... but Johnny committed suicide .... Long story.

I'm sorry to hear that.

Jolene is uncomfortable during the rest of her trip. She doesn't say a word to anyone and keeps it to herself.

The Jodi on the cruise does not know this information.... She thinks Clayton has fully taken Jodi's identity, possibly, but did Jodi take Clayton's identity as a child? Did he become a cop to conceal that identity? Her head hurts. She feels dizzy. Sick. She returns from the restroom on the beach and lounges in the chair while sipping on tea.

"How can I even bring this up?" She whispers to Alayna.

"Gregory came to help you but I don't believe he knows as much about Johnny either. Jodi always had a hard time talking about him… but I don't think he'll go as far as deluding himself."

"No, he hasn't, he's said Johnny committed suicide."

"Then he is Jodi …"

"No, the one on the phone."

Alayna gasps. "His brother is severely evil."

Jolene begins to panic.

"Stay calm, we are all here to help you."

"Please keep it quiet. I don't want anyone to know."

"Sure. No problem."

There is not much conversation between them from there. Jolene is highly suspicious. She makes her way home at the end of the cruise. She has the material she needs from the interviews to complete the articles for Vicky's magazine. She writes then she types – a habit of old fashion. She thinks about her journals; by now, she would have been working on her memoir but without her material she feels she's at the beginning all over again. She reflected on the beginning often in her memoir, preferring to begin with the end, and then come back to it again. Her style of writing is upon reflection. She has a newborn shoot tomorrow; she's a wreck. A manic mess. She closes her eyes then figures she needs to sit in the office. She needs to contemplate; she wants answers and feels stuck between a rock and a hard place. She moves toward her office and cuts a hard right to her private studio. She puts the room together for her early morning newborn shoot and pulls out wraps – blue, gray and white are the colors her client selected for their one week old baby boy. She places the floor mats, the props, the blankets and the accessories and the lighting where she needs them and then she closes the door; she is finished. Feeling ready she enters the office and sits behind her belated husband's desk – then she sobs – if he were alive she would not be going through this. Then her baby kicks. And she thinks of Dillon – how he would tell her everything will be all right. How he would embrace her in his masculine arms. Like Jodi. Like the man she feels is Jodi – when she reaches for a deeper place in her psyche. He doesn't feel right. She thinks she should have been reaching deeply sooner. Her intuition knows. She has to feel her way to the truth. She then enters the guest room.

"I have an early morning shoot and will need the house quiet," she says.

He rolls over in bed and turns away from the TV, "No problem, I'll be out for a while in the morning."

"Okay," she says but she doesn't ask where he is going because she'll be going to the condo. Her intuition is a guiding force, and she follows her instincts. She contemplates the truth; Jodi lied all those years ago and blamed Clayton for something he did? This is where she needs to lose the mind and find the heart; is Jodi a bullied youth who testified against his own brother and now he's a uniformed police officer? She sees how that scenario could have its repercussions. She stops thinking. She begins feeling. Her mind is confused but her heart is sound. She reflects again on her past then she bursts into tears again. She wants her husband and her old life back when his picture falls from the table. She looks up – what the hell was that? She is quiet. She looks at the window asserting that the window is not open. She picks up the broken pieces and glass falls upon her toes. She looks down and behind their photo are a key, a one-hundred dollar bill, and a note. She is in awe of the situation. She takes the key and reads: 110 Sunset Blvd. Then she opens the note and reads there: *To my beloved wife on her birthday...* she instinctively knows this is for her fortieth birthday and feels her husband had something planned for them. She wonders why there is a one hundred dollar bill. She places it into her purse and takes a shower. She is eager for the morning. More eager for the afternoon and most eager for the morning. She puts on her pajamas and slides her legs beneath the sheets. She turns off the bedside lamp and the darkness puts her at ease. She dreams of warm weather and the light of day breaks through her window at early dawn and she wakes at six o'clock to begin her day. She checks the guest room, and Jodi has left. After breakfast, a light read and some final touches to her article, she grabs her purse and dresses quickly. She heads into the studio and clicks the light on when her clients knock upon the door; they are early, but she is ready.

Chapter Sixteen

"Hello," she says, "welcome."

Her guests are a family of five and their third, a newborn, is only a week old with siblings that are twelve and eight. She feels their warmth shining through; she thinks of her own baby nestled deep within her stomach. She has a sonogram pending; they want to check the baby's weight. She dotes on her client's life – they seem to have it together. She and Dillon would have had it together, too. She's in love with her prospects – but is she fooling herself? The mother is Kimberly Webber – a super model. Jolene knows her body will mend soon, her bump is so small, and it will be unnoticed in a matter of weeks. She thinks about her baby's birth date and hopes that perhaps he'll be born in October as opposed to the first week in November – then her baby would have the same birth month as Gwynn's Henley. She wonders if Hudson is too similar of a name. She stops her mind from rambling. She picks up the camera and she begins with mom and snaps some shots. Kimberly stands at six feet tall with long limbs and slender legs. She had her first baby at the age of twenty-nine. Her husband Chris is equally beautiful. They are a stunning couple. Jolene adds the rest of the family to the photos; the baby startles and she rubs her finger over his face to soothe him. His name is Kingston and he does well for the sleeping baby photos. She molds his body into a froggy-pose and snaps the shots. Her session is two hours long and she does only one newborn shoot a day. After their session is over she picks up the props and cleans her studio; she takes to the computer and does some edits and sends some shots to the new mother. Then she sends the remaining bill for the session; she'll have the thirty proofs ready within the week.

Jolene takes a shower. She dresses casually and takes a deep breath. She looks inside the guest room to find that Jodi is still gone. She then dials the number from the key she is holding. The phone stops ringing and a receptionist picks up the call: *hello and thank you for calling – your storage solutions are with us...* it's an automated service. She presses prompt one for the address and jots it down. When she hangs up, she grabs Cash and her purse and heads out the door. Thirty minutes later she arrives at her destination and finds a storage unit. Her heart is racing – why didn't she know about this? Inside she finds the belongings that used to be in their garage; he didn't want to part with all that old sports equipment ... everything is packed in there but she looks down and inside a laundry basket is a box with her name engraved on the top along with a card: *I put this here in case she was right...* the note began.

Jolene,

Today I was found by a psychic. This woman came up to me at a game and told me something I could never forget; she pulled me to the side and said the infamous words... ask your wife who killed Kimberly.

Her jaw drops. Then she too drops to the floor as she continues to read.

Please forgive me for the mess in here. I kept these things to maybe one day pass them on to a son or a daughter of our own.

Jolene sheds tears and they drip down into a small pool just below the chin.

But then the psychic said something else.... You don't make it to your fortieth birthday, I'm afraid.

Jolene thinks of how wrong she was ... Dillon passed away at forty-one, but still, and she thinks what else could she be wrong about?

Her name is Nancy Crew and she is a psychic, or claims to be one. So if I'm no longer here then know that I am sorry.

The letter ends there. Jolene wipes her tears. She stands up and takes the lock box in her hands; it is full of playing cards. Collectors items. She thinks of how much she would like to pass those items to Hudson... and something inside her breaks. She feels angry in the moment: *Why!* She shouts, and she looks at all the sports equipment knowing that today she cannot take those items home but she will eventually ... and for certain her son can inherit these things. She closes the door to the storage shed and enters her car, turns on the ignition and speeds off – destined for the condo but she does not know why – does Sam live there? Did he inherit more than the truck? She focuses intently on knowing more than what Jodi said and thinks to herself that Gregory must be on to something ... who is Johnny? And what happened to Johnny?

She comes to the parking garage and finds the red truck with Jodi's plates still attached to the rear bumper. She makes her way to the door and knocks hard. No answer.

Harder still. Then the door opens and standing there is a disheveled Jodi or Clayton … who she does not know.

"Clayton?" She is taken aback by his appearance.

He shuts the door to shield his tears. She can hear him sobbing through the door. When he opens the door he is wiping his face.

"It's Jodi, Jo. I'm Jodi. You know me…"

His appearance is distracting, obscuring his words. The question forms in her mind: Who killed Kimberly?

"Clayton?" She whispers.

His face is unshaved and his hair is wild. She pushes past him and enters the condo. She is unafraid. The condo is equally unkempt as he is.

"Jo, I would have called but I waited for you … the last time we spoke … you were to call me back. I never heard from you."

He shuts the door. The lighting is dim.

"He's taking my life from me," he says and on his ankle is a bracelet for those who are on probation.

"The Department isn't taking any chances," he flashes his foot, "So I have to wear this."

Jolene is speechless.

"Who the hell have I been with these past months?"

She is showing. He finally notices.

"Jo, you're pregnant?"

"Tell me," she speaks softly, "who is Johnny?"

He looks puzzled at first.

"He's an old friend. I helped him … but it wasn't enough. … He shot himself using his father's gun."

"Would Clayton know that?"

"No, Clayton was put away …."

"You could have called me."

"I know Jo, and I'm sorry … I thought you were done with me."

"It's a boy …"

She's not sure if she should be telling him.

"Tell me, how do you know Johnny… and …," he pauses, "is that my boy?"

"Yes."

"I thought I hadn't a reason to live anymore …"

"Gregory spoke of him."

"Greg knows me through and through … inside and out. I'm afraid I stopped taking calls."

"Why?"

"I can't live with all I know thinking I'm Clayton… he's been using my identity… I never knew what powerless was like before."

"Who killed Kimberly?"

"Not me, Jo. I swear."

"Did Clayton kill Kim? Did he steal my journals?"

"He's a manipulator, Jo... I don't know how he's getting away with this."

"Did you take a lie detector test?"

"They have one for me... my lawyer says it could help... a public defender."

"When do you take the test?"

"It's scheduled for next week."

Jolene scans the condo with her eyes. Everything is out of place. Out of character for Jodi. She is not convinced. She moves toward the back bedroom and finds an unkempt bed. She does not know who she has been living with for the past month.

"It's best to call after the test," she says, and she moves swiftly out of the room.

"I hope that you will let me see him."

"Who?" She is forgetful.

"Our son," he says, and she can take no more.

She flees through the front door and enters her car. She dials Adam and when he's on the line she requests to know about the lie detector test. He confirms for her that it is scheduled for next week. Satisfied she hangs up. She drives toward home. She enters the house and immediately goes to the guest room. She searches for anything that will tell her his identity. He had hardly left anything behind. She finds a duffle bag under the bed. She opens it and takes everything out: shirts, shorts, shoes and a single receipt. The receipt she reads is for a pawn shop; a single item was pawned it seems and the receipt reads *fine crystal*. She takes hold of the receipt and places everything else into the duffle bag. She enters the hallway and phones Adam again.

"I have something I want you to look into!"

She delivers the receipt. Adam unfolds the paper and looks to Jolene.

"Where did you get this?"

She tells him the receipt was found inside a duffle bag.

"He is living with you?" Adam asks.

"Yes. But Jodi, or hell, Clayton possibly, whoever, told me the receipt was in the trunk of the car."

"Is it possible the duffle bag was in the car? Did Clayton or Jodi know Kim?"

"I hadn't thought of that."

"Sounds suspicious, like one of them was keeping tabs on the place."

"What place?"

"Your place."

Now Jolene is frightened. She considers all that has happened and worries about her health and the well-being of the baby.

Adam heads downtown to where the crystal was pawned. He snaps a photograph and Jolene checks her mobile phone ... she is able to identify the crystal as being her own. She feels deceived and manipulated. Adam informs the worker that the crystal is stolen and Jolene files another report. The crystal is taken for evidence in the death of Kimberly Anne Turner. Adam forwards the photo to Jodi's public defender and the crystal is dusted for prints. In the couple weeks that go by, Jolene learns that the crystal was wiped clean by the staff and no prints were found.

"They cleaned it dry," Adam says over the phone.

Jolene feels she is at the beginning of a long obstacle course and she doesn't know if she can bear any more ... but now she owes her baby the knowledge of exactly who his father is. When Jodi returns home she is quiet. In her mind she is saying: Who is Clayton? But one of them had her crystal. It was one of a kind and had been given to her and Dillon as an anniversary gift; his mother collected fine crystal.

In the week that ensues, Adam delivers the message: *Jolene, they both passed the test. They claim to be the same person and they both passed the tests. There is a repeat test scheduled on another week.* Jolene has been keeping her distance from the twin brothers. They are either good manipulators or they both honestly believe what they are saying. Jolene heads back to the condo. She feels she can make ends-meet of this situation if she finds her heart.

"Hello," he says after peering through the peep hole. His eyes are reddened... has he been crying? He appears solemn. Her heart aches. This could be the father of her baby. Her abdomen is showing. He gets down on one knee and places his hands on each side of her abdomen. He cries into her stomach like burying his face into the smooth texture of cotton linen.

"I'm telling you the truth but I can't get anywhere, Jo," he says, and he's folding under the pressure. She takes him by the hand.

"If you're Jodi, remind me ... what happened to Johnny?"

"I tried to help him, but he took his father's gun, and he shot himself...," a voice from behind her shoulder says. Jodi, from inside the condo, stands to his feet.

"Clayton," he says, "why are you doing this? They let you go free..."

"You are mistaken, brother ... when you took my name and claimed your innocence!"

Jodi's red eyes show pain and he looks sternly into his brother's face, "You believe I killed our school teacher?"

"No, brother. You are the one that killed her, and then took my name! Took my life!"

"I took nothing from you."

Jolene moves backwards out from between them. She looks

left at his earnest face. Those tears. A police officer down the beaten path. She looks right at the stern look of a man whose allegations will be heard – and how the hell to discern the truth, she thinks. She wants to run but her feet won't move as if they're planted to the floor. She feels heavy on legs that feel as though they could collapse under the pressure. All her avenues of discerning the truth have hit a road block and she wonders what to do next – DNA says one of them killed Martha Cohen, but has the wrong brother served a vicious sentence for something he did not do?

"Jo, I want to help you raise this baby." He's almost pleading. He breaks her concentration and her thought processes turn to the unborn child – then she runs. She flees from a demise that overwhelms her. She enters the elevator and heads out into the open air of one of the hottest days in the month; it is August and she has clients booked for weeks but she is distracted. She phones Adam.

"Hello?" He knows her number.

"I need some help … some personal help … I want to change locks to the house."

She did not know who else to call. She doesn't want to alarm anyone. She thinks of her sister – what would she think of all this? Her mind veers to Jared – if only her life could be that normal. She goes to the hardware store and with some help from a clerk she buys new door knobs and when she arrives home Adam is there to greet her. Together they remove the old knobs and affix the new ones; once all the doors are changed, Adam renders a mock salute and moves out the front door and tests the keys. When all works well he gives her a firm handshake and a comforting smile. She salutes him back and they both laugh – she needs the comedic relief.

She enters her study and closes the doors. She takes a look at her deceased husband's large oak desk and she has a seat in his leather bound chair. She swivels to look outside and a tear streaks her face. She receives a text from Vicki: *Thinking of you.* And she responds: *I'll have the article posted in a day.* In addition to the magazine, Vicki is creating a blog and a website so Jolene's articles from the magazine will be partially featured online. Vicky is pleased with Jolene's work but she responds: *Well I didn't mention the article.* Jolene texts back: *I know, and I'm thinking of you too...* Vicky doesn't know much from the last three weeks. Jolene has been staying busy with clients and her mind has been a whirlwind. She turns to face the desk and with a sigh she opens the drawers to the desk... and there they are. Four journals placed neatly into the drawer as if they had been there the whole time. Her hands shake and she thinks only of Clayton.... *Where did you get my journals?* It does not take long for him to respond... *Your Jodi's condo... they were in that hell hole among the rubbish. He's a liar and a fake.* And she blocks his call. She wants no more of this ... at this moment, she's done with the mind games. She texts Jodi: *You delivered my journals?*

He does not text back until late into the evening: *Jo, I haven't seen them. I can't look into it with all that is happening ... please understand* ... and she turns the phone off and turns in for the night.

Chapter Seventeen

Jolene awakens to the sun glaring off the window pane. She goes to her phone – most things can be done with a smart phone. She searches Nancy Crew, the psychic. She is taken to a social media page and Nancy appears as a small, petite woman with long, wavy white hair, wearing a floral dress. Jolene sends a message: *Do you remember Dillon?* She presses send knowing she's likely not giving enough information. The site says she usually responds within 24 hours. She dresses simply in a sheer shirt and jean shorts; her client is due in at nine o'clock in the morning – another newborn shoot. She is nervous she'll see Jodi or Clayton, and she welcomes the clients as a distraction from her complicated life. The client's baby is named Treasure, a boy, and Jolene thinks it's a neat name. She goes into photographer mode and she takes them into her studio. She closes the door. The room is dimly lit and it is warm inside. She swaddles the baby in a wrap and places him in a basket of blue, beige and gray linen. He is asleep. She feels the kicking of her own baby remembering her sonogram is today – and she'll be alone, or at best, she'll invite Vicky.

After the photo shoot she sends a message to Gwyneth: *Just checking on you ... great pics on social media last night!* Gwyneth shared her sonogram photos including the gender reveal as she is more certain now that she is showing better. At six months pregnant, she has gained weight and she shares her smooth abdomen – she is happy and feeling blessed to have a baby – the boy they had tried for years to have. Jolene caresses her abdomen and checks her phone; she has received a message from the psychic: *No, I sure don't.* Jolene reminds her and writes verbatim from Dillon's letter. Then Nancy replies that Dillon had an aura of grave danger. She asks how he is doing. *Dead.* Jolene is morose. Nancy writes her a tender letter about the death of her own husband and how she, as a sensitive, knew of his death as well - *he had a massive stroke,* she says and Jolene feels no better. But what else could the psychic tell her? *Are you a medium?* Jolene writes. *I can channel their energy but I don't claim to be able to do so.* Now she is confusing to Jolene. She schedules a personal meeting with Nancy for later that day as her needs sound urgent. When Jolene arrives at her destination in San Diego she comes to a small store and office where she is burning incense and a doorway is covered by a blue tapestry with the moon, the sun and stars on it. Jolene pries open the curtain to find a round table complete with a gazing crystal; Nancy is short, plump and busty. She wears a long fish-net like sweater over flowing slacks and a silky shirt. She asks Jolene to enter and has passion in her eyes.

"We have both lost our husbands," she says while Jolene takes a seat, "but you have even more troubles don't you?"

"I don't know who killed Kim," she says and her voice is sullen. She'll take just about any advice at this point.

Nancy takes a seat opposite of Jolene and she glares intentionally at the orb before her.

"There are not one but two men in your life I see...," she nods knowingly, "there is great conflict surrounding you ... surrounding these men. I see the same face in both of them but their energy is very different …"

"Yes," Jolene is hopeful.

"There is a woman … she is confused. Her mind isn't so good …"

"Marlena?"

"From this woman you could dig deeper into her, into her possessions, into her estate…"

"I never thought of that…"

"There may be something there that will be valuable to you."

"What is it?"

"I'm sorry but it is not clear."

"Thank you… you have helped me greatly, now, but you couldn't help my husband…"

"Nor my own," Nancy rubs the top of Jolene's hand.

Jolene places cash upon the table and makes her exit. Her drive is prolonged in heavy traffic. She drives toward the condo. Toward Jodi. Praying she has the right one. She pleads into the open air: *Let me be right*. She thinks.

An hour later, Jodi opens the door. His eyes are encased with dark circles.

"Help me …," then her voice cracks. She doesn't want to take a chance and she re-thinks her strategy.

"I'm going to help you find the truth," she says, and he hugs her.

"I miss our life, Jo." And she pats his back and once he lets go she makes an exit.

"I miss you so much," he says, and she enters the elevator and the doors close behind her. Her thoughts are on Marlena. She wants to visit before there's no more time. She checks her schedule and makes haste during visiting hours ... but she knows she'll need documentation. She contacts Adam who puts her in touch with her attorney. She gathers some belongings and decides to stay overnight at a hotel. In the morning she'll tend to her photo shoot and submit the finished articles for Vicky. She takes the stairs when she arrives at the law office. She enters the small and cluttered reception area and the receptionist calls her by name.

"Yes," Jolene says.

"He says these are for a friend."

"Thank you," she says and she leaves the office without ever seeing the attorney Michael Frederick.

Jolene heads north. The traffic is congested. She checks in at the hotel and decides to move the appointment to the afternoon and sends a message to the client. She pours herself a glass of water and turns on the coffee maker. She slips off her shoes and pulls a silk shirt over her head, her hair thrown into a bun, and slips on a pair of cotton shorts. She finds her phone at the bottom of her purse and there are multiple messages on her phone. She listens to each one. Jodi is phoning her and wants to meet. The Jodi she knows won't leave the condo. She stands firm on her sentiments and rejects the call, then adds a block to the number. She texts Jodi: *What else can you tell me that only you (we) know.*

He responds within the hour, "I know intimacy ...." Something I hope he cannot tell you…"

She quickly adds: *No, he cannot.*

She then proceeds to tell him more about the baby while still keeping their communications light and easy. She jokes about putting "nothing in the vagina" and he laughs, too – the comedic relief is beneficial in that moment.

Had my second lie detector test this afternoon…

Oh, yeah?

I'm still not lying, Jo.

The problem is that test says he's not either.

He's a manipulator.

I'm turning in. Talk soon.

And she doesn't respond as he writes. *Good night.*

She feels her heart is with the officer of the law … she reaches deep within to decide he is genuine – or maybe she's just out for proof and the truth shall reveal itself. She knows what she needs to do … before anyone else can. Before Clayton can get to her first. She gathers the legal document – a living will – and heads on the interstate toward the nursing home. She sends silent prayers that she is not too late. She arrives fifteen minutes later and she signs her name to the visiting board. She finds Marlena in her room, who is receiving a sponge bath, and she waits outside the door. Clearly the psychic is right and Marlena is not in an urn. She is alive but not well. Jodi, who may have been Clayton was lying.

When the nurse exits she says, "She's alert today," and Jolene smiles, "must be because you're here."

"Thank you." She says, thinking it must be a sign.

"Hello, Marlena," Jolene says and she takes a seat aside her as she peers out the window.

"Do I know you?" Marlena is frank.

"I am Jodi's fiancée and I'm trying to help him."

"Is he in some kind of trouble?"

"Yes, he is," Jolene wonders how she remembers him today.

"Well, then help him. I obviously can't." She is candid and turns her face from Jolene and begins to whistle while glaring outside again.

"Do I know you?" Her face is flat.

"Yes, you do. I'm having your son's baby."

"What do you want from me?"

"Your signature and your blessing."

"Sign what?"

"A living will, so Jodi can have his memories."

"Memories?"

"Like family photos."

"Oh."

Jolene unfolds the document and places it onto a clipboard that hangs from the wall.

"Can you sign this form?"

"Will it get rid of you?"

"Yes."

With a shaky hand she takes the pen and scribbles her name in a fine, yet legible print.

"Did I spell that right?"

"Yes, you did."

"Get my nurse." Marlena folds her hands in her lap, and Jolene has to take the clipboard from her hands and she tucks the papers away in her purse.

"I can do that for you." She says as she stands, "Thank you, Marlena."

She finally looks up, quizzically, "Huh? You're not my nurse…"

The nurse walks in yielding a mobile cart and administers medication as Jolene quietly leaves the room. Her thoughts are on the uniformed officer who pulled her over last December. She thinks of him and hopes she is right. She takes the document to get it notarized and she has to find out what belongings are being left behind. She wonders if Nancy Crew can also envision lost artifacts.

She chuckles faintly into her hand until she thinks of Dillon wishing she knew then what the psychic told her husband. Wishing she could save him. But she couldn't. Maybe she can save Jodi… maybe Clayton's soul. She returns home and lets Cash out. She goes into the back yard and dips her feet in the pool. She pours herself a glass of peach flavored tea and turns on somber music that takes her mind to a different place – Dillon loved soft classical music. It was his style that was so charming. He wanted Bach over contemporary artists. She loved him. She misses his biscuits and gravy and would give anything to touch him, but when the baby kicks she is taken out of reverie and is in the present moment. She caresses her abdomen and sends a loving message to her sister: *We need to get them together often*, followed by a heart emoji. She yearns for family. She is without parents and without a husband. She considers how fast the months are passing and she feels like perhaps her life is rushed – if she were not so hasty maybe she wouldn't be in the predicament. She cannot help but to feel the intensity of remorse. She wants salvation for the one who did not place the pencil in Mrs. Cohen's neck – and that should be her Jodi. She is interrupted by the message: *We will. On every holiday and the weekends when we catch a break.*

Jolene smiles. *That's a deal*, she types and thinks of her sister as the most adoring person. Her mind then shifts to Kim. *Poor Kim*, she thinks. She considers the fact that she owes Kim too; she owes her killer. Jolene feels nervous. The psychic knew then long before it happened and that being the case – why doesn't she know who killed Kim? Jolene drinks from her glass and steps into the pool with the water up to her knees. She is alone. When alone her mind wonders; she finally stopped having nightmares of the crash, but now her life is one long continuous nightmare. She feels as though she is living a movie no one is watching.

She hears a knock on the front door. Subtle at first. Then harder. She gazes through the peep hole and finds Clayton, not Jodi, who she found is too sullen... she speaks through the door.

"I'm not letting you in."

He steps back. "Come on, Jo. You know it's me... it's me all along... he's a fake and a liar. He's done this for years, Jo. Since we were kids."

When did he start calling her Jo? Her mind wonders.

"I just want to be left alone."

"You can't raise the baby alone, Jo."

She is alarmed by his tenacity and thinks he's never going away. She takes Cash and slips out the back door. She starts her car and exits the driveway. She phones Vicky, who is not home, and considers the condo ... and that's where she goes. He opens the door; his world is upside down as if his own brother has broken him. She steps inside and he puts his arms around her and his head on her shoulder.

"They think I have killed her," he says and Jolene holds him. "He just won't fail the lie detector test."

"I have something," she says, and he lets go of their

embrace. She opens the paper and shows him his mother's confirmation of a living will. She has left Jodi

her assets and Jolene asks where such items would be located. He does not know where such belongings would be located. He assumed all their belongings were thrown out when she was placed in the retirement home. Jolene says okay, and doesn't push for any more answers. She feels the loss at the pit of her stomach.

"Where is your father?" She asks, and he shakes his head in disgust.

"In a filthy trailer somewhere north of here."

She thinks he must be in Northern California then, and the reason his mother is where she is located.

"We need to find him. We need to find out if he has any of your belongings." Jodi doesn't know what she is up to because he is not all there. He is half listening like a broken man. She makes her way into the living room.

"He returned my journals."

"He's taken my name. My life. He's saying he is me…"

"He said you had taken my journals."

"Of course he did."

"How would he know where to put them?"

"Where did he, Jo?"

"In the desk drawer."

"And the duffle bag?"

"Had the receipt for the crystal."

"That should be enough evidence."

"But it isn't. And he returned them. So they are technically no longer stolen."

"How does he figure he can get away with this?"

"How does he pass a lie detector test?" Jolene makes a point.

"He's delusional. He believes his own story."

"We have to convince the court that you are not lying."

"We have to convince the court of more than that."

"But he has to convince them, too."

Jolene considers another thought, "He's fooled me once," she says, "he won't fool me again."

"We need to get you put back together," Jolene says, "I need you to be well."

"The stress is going to kill me."

"It won't … and we need to locate your father."

"What are you after?"

"Everything from birth."

"You want our identities."

"Yes."

"Makes sense."

Jodi jots down his father's last known address and Jolene puts the paper into her purse. She may have to go alone. Jodi is virtually on house arrest wearing an ankle bracelet – a new California law for someone pending a trial – so they don't go AWOL; it's that or sit it out in prison. Jolene leaves for the evening. She has a client in the early afternoon and afterwards she's hoping to take a trip. She returns home and finds a message from Vicky: *Love the articles*, she says and Jolene thinks about the cruise liner and how they both seemed perfectly normal. But one of them is lying. She feels the intensity of the situation in her stomach. To de-stress she makes an herbal tea and takes a hot bath. She soaks with a coconut scented bath bomb. She thinks this situation is a day closer to being normal and she closes her eyes and lets the music penetrate her soul.

Chapter Eighteen

She opens her eyes in the morning with the TV left on. She gets dressed in something comfortable and makes a cup of coffee. She takes Cash into the yard. The day is bright; no sign of rain. She intends to go north for the day once she finishes with her client; she has a birthday party to attend. She is not in the party mood but work is work. She heads north for the party – a total convenience. When she arrives she is greeted by the mother, Peggy Simpson, and her daughter, a sweet sixteen, is mingling with friends. Their back yard is expansive and equipped with a luxurious pool and hot tub. Jolene turns on her digital camera and gets some early photos of Annabelle-Rose acting naturally among friends. Jolene stays with the party for two hours and has the photos in the end to highlight those precious memories; she films her face when presented with a new car; a contemporary four wheel SUV. Fully loaded. Annabelle-Rose is pictured with tears of happiness streaming down her thin face. Life for them is good.

Jolene packs her car and stops at the gas station. She grabs a snack and a cola, and heads north. She follows the Google map north of San Francisco. The house she comes to is not a trailer. Was Jodi wrong? Or did his father move? The home is small and plain. White. No shutters. She steps onto the concrete slab outside of the house and touches the rusted railing hoping not to get an infection – it disintegrates softly in her fingers. She rubs the shards off on her blue jean capris. When she knocks she can hear movement inside. She is now nervous. What is she doing? She takes a step back as the door opens and she finds a man, not the deadbeat she pictured, who is aged but well-kept and clean.

"Hello," she says, not certain what else to say, "I'm here about Jodi." She hopes she said the right name.

"You want to come on inside?"

Her nerves are flinching.

"I was hoping to talk with you ..." she stays put outside.

"Come on in here and I'll get us something to drink."

She shuffles through the door with quick little steps - she's an anxious mess.

"Don't be nervous," he notices, "I'm not going to bite you."

"Thank you," she says and she finds the home is sparse and simple. There are no empty beer cans strewn about. They have a seat at the kitchen table.

"Jodi may have told you about me," he says, looking troubled, "I was a different man back then. A drunk." He is frank.

"You were physical with your boys?"

"Only when they were out of line back then. Mostly Clayton. He was always pushing our buttons so-to-speak."

"How bad were the beatings?"

"They got the belt when they were out of line."

"It's likely I had Clayton living in my house ... he's claiming to be Jodi..."

"That wouldn't surprise me any... uh... what did you say your name was?"

"It's Jolene. Why do you say that?"

"Clayton had troubles. Marlena told him frequently she had only one son."

"What kind of troubles?"

"All kinds. He didn't listen. He was causing issues with others besides his mother and I ... he would concoct traps around the house ... used my nail gun once ... said he'd kill people who didn't listen. He was an odd boy to most other boys... he often wondered if he could disassemble animals and learn how they worked. A neighborhood girl told him to become a veterinarian while some just said he's disturbing. We never knew what was wrong with him."

"Did Jodi get beatings?"

"They both did. When they were out of line."

"Did it happen often? I mean every day or ...."

"Clayton more than Jodi."

"Can you tell them apart? I mean, do they have birthmarks or ..."

"I wouldn't know, Jolene. We just weren't close. Marlena would know more than I."

"Her mind isn't strong much anymore."

"I see."

"Would you possibly have childhood items still in this house?"

"Everything got stored in the attic. Haven't been up there in years."

"Is this their childhood home?"

"It was for Jodi. Moved here after the school incident. Marlena didn't want problems for Jodi so we moved."

"Would you mind if I take a look in the attic?"

"Sure. Take what you want. If Jodi wants to have it."

"Thank you ... where do I go?"

They enter the hallway and he pulls the door opening to the attic. Jolene thanks him again and she makes her way up the stairs. She peers at boxes upon boxes. She tells him she needs to rent a truck to take the boxes. He agrees with her and they arrange a day next week when she can unload the boxes from the attic. In the meantime, she sets up four more shoots to be done outdoors and one studio session for a newborn. She does not hear from Jodi so she makes the call; when he has answered the phone she tells him of her progress. He does not believe she can find anything useful but he stifles his doubts and thanks her. She is now working with his depression; he is letting his brother win in this way, she thinks. She tells him not to get so down. He says his life is in shambles because he has a brother who not only couldn't follow the laws but has deep-rooted issues. When she tells him about the girl from the neighborhood he says that was Alayna ... and she didn't know they go that far back.

"Why didn't you tell me?" She is annoyed.

"Because that wasn't me that time," he says, "you have been with Clayton," and his voice cracks. "Thinking about you with him kills me." Jolene can feel the damage at the pit of her stomach.

"We didn't have sex. And he stayed in the guest room."

"Still." He says flatly.

"I know…"

"He's taking my life."

Then there is a long pause on the line as if the call has ended. She wonders if there is a dropped call when he gets back onto the line.

"I can't wait to see you again," he says, and she feels some reservation. Something amiss. Something odd.

"I have my sonogram tomorrow," she says.

"But you've already done that."

"It's my advanced age. And they want to check his weight."

"I can't believe I'm going to be a father," she hears a glimmer of hope in his voice when she begins to hear the shouting of someone else.

"Jo," he yells from the background, "he's lying, Jo...."

And she hears the commotion of rambling between two people that can only mean both Jodi and Clayton are in the same room. She ends the call. Quickly she is in contact with his father.

"I need to come soon," she says, uncertain what else she can do, so she calls the police and reports the commotion claiming there is a domestic violence case and a disturbance coming from within the condo. She rents a truck with enough space for the boxes and heads north hoping the police can handle the disturbance inside the condo. When she arrives, he opens the door and he can see the look of terror on her face.

"Is something wrong?"

"No...," she says, saving herself some time. He is elderly and feeble so she takes the boxes, one at a time, lugging them down the stairs and into the truck. Two hours later she heads home. She says a silent prayer and wishes Jodi would follow up but she does not get a call. She sends a heartfelt text: *Are you alone?*

Fifteen minutes later she receives the response: *No.* She senses urgency and she flees toward the condo then she re-thinks and sends another message: *Who is with you?* She does not receive a response. A woman crosses her mind and she feels going there will resolve some pent-up problems. Why hadn't Jodi gotten in touch with her if in fact Clayton was staying in the guest room? Her heart is racing when she knocks on the door. She hears commotion inside but no one answers the door. She sends another text: *I can hear you inside.* Still, no one answers. She checks the door knob and it turns. She enters the foyer and peers around the first corner when she hears his voice.

"What are you doing here?"

"Come to help you...

"You can't help me," he says in a low monotone.

"Yes, I can."

"Court is tomorrow. I'm up for murder in the first degree... a man in uniform, my uniform, killed Kimberly, and that guy looks like me."

"Pun intended?"

"This is no time for jokes."

"No I'm serious... he does look like you ... wearing your uniform."

"How would he have gotten my uniform?"

"He's been coming into the condo, Jodi ..."

"He had your journals, your crystal for money, all wearing my uniform?"

"Yes."

"You know I just thought of something..."

Jodi takes his phone from his pocket and dials a number. When someone answers he responds, "I think I've left my uniforms there under Jodi McCain?" He is put on hold. When the clerk returns he nods to Jolene in confirmation then hangs up.

"Jo, I never picked up my dry cleaning."

"So you're saying..."

"She said I already picked up my dry cleaning ... I forgot... until now. I never went because I was with you and forgot ... then I went to jail."

"Clayton claimed your identity and took your uniform."

"He's posing as me, Jo. My twin brother wants to take my life from me."

"This is good for court..."

"My public defender ..."

"Yes, he can help you. This is good evidence that Clayton is stealing your identity."

"There has to be proof."

"Reasonable doubt."

Jolene tells him about his father and Jodi is reserved; he still feels the pain in his back from his father and talks of the scars to prove it; the lacerations in his back are from the belt.

"We both have the scars," Jodi says.

"I never noticed them," Jolene is uneasy.

He removes his shirt and drops his briefs. There are scars across his lower back.

"Nothing a pair of shorts can't cover up."

Jolene feels foolish – she learns all this while pregnant, like a teenager but she shrugs it off.

"I have my sonogram," she says, "do you want to go?"

"Yes," he says, and she manages a smile.

Jolene drives. She is in the truck and could use his help after the appointment. While there they sit at Maternal Fetal Medicine for fifteen minutes when they are called back. She removes her slacks and takes a seat on the exam chair and lays back. The sonogram tech places warm jelly on her abdomen and begins the session. She locates the face, the heart, the spine, the right hand, both feet and the gender. Jodi sees his son for the first time and Jolene squeezes his hand; she can see the sparkle in his eye. Once again they feel normal. Jodi wants his life back and Jolene senses this. After twenty minutes the doctor enters the room and tells her the placenta has moved over the cervix where it should be and is therefore resolved and the baby has gained weight. All is good and they are thankful. Jolene tells him of her upcoming appointments but she wants to cancel to go through the boxes.

"Don't cancel, I will help you," he says and she places her arms around his neck. She drives home and together they unload the boxes. There are many to go through and they search the artifacts for anything from birth: baseball cards, team jerseys, collector coins and old photos. So far there is nothing that can help them identify which twin was birthed with what name. Jolene lets him crash on the couch. She retreats to her room and locks the door. Into the night, Jodi hears something from outside the window and moves toward the glass to peer into the street; he sees no one but in the morning the truck has a flat from a nail and Jolene is held back from continuing her obligation to return the truck until it is fixed. Jodi takes on that obligation while Jolene does a photo shoot inside her studio. The newborn sleeps; she gives her a bottle in between poses. She gets pooped on while Jodi changes the tire for the spare. When all is wrapped up and finished, Jolene cleans up and together they return the truck. Jolene climbs into the passenger side of his truck after paying for the tire and they return home when Jolene lets out a scream and Jodi looks astonished; her house is in flames. The firemen work vigorously to put out the fire. She cries in disbelief as her home swelters in the flames. Jodi puts his arms around her to keep her from going inside when she yells frantically for Cash.

"Jo, I know I let him outside … I may not have let him back in." Jolene runs to the side of the house where she finds frantic Cash cowering beneath a rose bush. She scoops him up into her arms and cries into his fur. Jodi gets down on one knee.

"This is all my fault," he says, "you're going through this because of me."

"It's not your fault," she says when a fireman approaches them, and she sits on the ground letting Jodi hold her.

"It may have been rats," the fireman says, "There are some exposed wires in your cellar." Officer O'Neil is on the scene. Jodi approaches his old partner, "Do you have a reason to suspect arson?" Jodi tries to remain calm. The bones in his body tell him there is something more.

"Not by what they can tell." Officer O'Neil is calm, "I want you to know the precinct is rooting for you, Jodi," she says. Jodi nods, "That's good to know, Susie." She flashes him a smile but she feels the concern. "They say the wires were wonky in the junction box, too," she further tries to lessen the need for fear.

"I don't want to alarm, Jolene," he says lowly.

"I understand." She says, "There may not be any concern," but she is uncertain.

The fire sparked interest from the media; cameras capture the fire and the TV reporter spots Jodi.

"Mr. McCain... do you have reason to believe foul play?" He wanted the conversation to go smoother than this. He does not respond. He takes Jolene by the hand and together they try to view what may be left; her journals are now charred, her studio is ashes, and the boxes she had taken from his childhood home appear to be incinerated.

"We have insurance," he tries to console her but she is taken to her knees and she sobs.

The Friday morning headline reads: *Fire Strikes in the McCain Case* and Jolene is mortified. She always had been a private person but now her life is news for the media. She feels the depths of failure — the hope depletes in her body. She receives a call from a client that morning who cancels her wedding photo shoot: *I don't want my family involved with all that drama*, she says boldly and Jolene feels the angst of the situation — losing a client she takes personal, and now she fumes inside to no relief. She gives in to a degree; her mind shutting down, she wants to call it quits ... if it wasn't for a baby ... but she doesn't want pity and thinks that perhaps there's a glimmer of light at the end of this immensely dark tunnel. She doesn't know where to turn other than to Vicky and Gwyneth: *My house burned but I am fine*, is all she could say, and when her phone rings she answers and it's Gwyneth who sounds alarmed.

Chapter Nineteen

She goes with him to the condo; she is in all the way with him. This is now their problem together. Her sister doesn't agree and wants Jolene to move to Montana, but Jolene is a fighter - she's already lost one – and she doesn't want to lose another.

"Jodi," she says, "we're in this together now." She firmly stands her ground.

"If he is lying," Jolene tells her sister, "then Clayton belongs in jail."

"But what if Clayton is not lying?" Gwyneth pleads.

"I had the evidence…" her voice cracks, "but I'm defeated by that fire."

"No, you're not." Gwyneth is reassuring to her, "You are not defeated even if Jodi is …"

"But that's not fair," Jolene argues and she tells her sister she loves her and she ends the call hoping on good terms but understanding her sister has nothing but love for her.

"Why do you suspect arson?" Jolene is stern.

Jodi takes one look at her face and can tell he cannot lie, "The nail in the tire … it's suspicious…"

"If someone put that nail in the tire and wanted to prevent us from leaving the house?"

"You're very smart, Jolene."

"You suspect Clayton is doing this?"

"He knows every step we take…"

"How?"

"Maybe there's someone he's paying…"

"A hitman?"

"I think perhaps something like that, but of course I'm not sure."

"You think he was trying to kill us?"

"We already know he's capable of murder."

"What makes a man kill?"

"A dark sense of things around him."

"He's crazy."

"That was the verdict, so he went to the juvenile detention facility. They transferred him to the psychiatric ward nearly the same time as my mother."

"What was wrong with her?"

"My father made her go crazy. She couldn't deal with life anymore."

"Jodi," she thinks calmly, "do you know of any identifying birthmarks between you and your brother?"

"Clayton has one. I don't have them. We used to joke it was the size of Texas."

"Where?"

"It's on his leg. It's white. Doesn't tan so we could really see it in the summer."

Jolene is wishing she asked him from the beginning.

"Why does your mother say Jodi has the birthmark? She says Jodi is her only son."

"She's confused. She's done that since we were kids. Always had us confused... I blame the booze and my father."

"Did she drink?"

"No, only my father."

Jolene turns her attention back to the ash and they leave in Jodi's truck and find the fire is out. She wishes she could turn back the hands of time; she wishes to see her home in one piece. With the fire out they look through the rubbish; only half the house has burned: the studio, the office, the master bedroom, but not the guest room and only part of the living and family room. The boxes were near the front entrance and most of them have been spared. Since they bring back Jodi's truck they load those boxes and the clothes stored in the laundry room since most of the master bedroom burned and fill the truck with everything salvaged from the rubbish. Jolene stifles her tears thinking she is just content with the fact that her baby is safe; they are safe. They turn away from the debris and head back to the condo; they unload the truck and from then on Jolene thinks about revenge in whatever form it takes to bring down a ruthless criminal. Jodi explains that Officer O'Neil is overseeing his case at the precinct but due to discrimination and bias the case is being turned over to a Sergeant Harris who is new at the precinct and doesn't know Jodi personally. That's when Jolene tells him about Adam and Jodi looks impressed and hurt at the same time that she could not trust him or tell him apart from his sick and deranged brother. Jolene does not know how one twin can be so evil but again that is something Jodi blames on his father – his belligerence made the family go crazy. Now it's Clayton who is out for revenge against a brother who told the truth all those years ago: Clayton McCain stabbed his school teacher in the throat with a pencil. Jodi was the only witness. Now after all those years Clayton takes the identity of the innocent brother and wrecks his life. But what she knows doesn't matter; what matters is what they agree to within court and that means they need to go to the table with hard evidence. Jolene is tired but she thinks this story is unfolding for her and she doesn't want to let him go to jail for murder in the first degree in the death of Kimberly; Kimberly deserves justice and the true killer must be sent to prison. She rummages through the boxes unable to sleep. She finds old photos for sure but nothing that can identify Jodi apart from his twin brother Clayton. She finds old Christmas cards, stockings, lights and more miscellaneous junk. She finds collector cards and more cars and a baseball trophy with Jodi's name written in bronze. They had a life away from their parents and she ponders why one would turn vicious while the other becomes an officer of the law – what a difference in the two of them and yet she does not know how this scenario will play out in court and they only have a week. She feels the feet of her growing baby inside her abdomen. She is momentarily subdued by the thoughts of having a baby in her arms in two months-time.

"A motion for continuation and postponement," Jodi says and he informs her he just spoke with his public defender.

Jolene wonders how her husband could have helped someone like him. She hopes a public defender can be equally as strong within a courtroom; how will his public defender hold up to Clayton's lawyer. Are they going to prove Clayton is Jodi? Jodi stole his identity as a child to avoid punitive measures? Perhaps now they can seek the psychiatrist in Clayton's case and Jolene phones Adam. He does not answer but his receptionist schedules her an appointment to see Adam in person. She wants to get to the bottom of this disaster and she finds a box of files from the case of Mrs. Cohen and her unfortunate death; the files are in folder files from the attorney's office. Right then and there, Jolene finds a piece of evidence she desperately needs in that moment: the name of the psychiatric doctor who examined Clayton, and her name is Barbara McConnell. Jolene turns to her phone to research the medical professional on the web and she locates the name of the woman who now has her own practice. Jolene looks out to the starlit sky and imagines Dillon overseeing her and she feels like an angel put that box there where she could see to it first thing.

She phones Barbara's business and she leaves a detailed message, then Jolene tells Jodi to phone his lawyer and request the records are relinquished for court purposes.

"There will be documents to sign to release that

information as it's protected by HIPPA," Jolene says, "everyone has a right to privacy."

"I'll see what she can do," Jodi says, and he looks over a small album of photos realizing there were good times with his family too, and he feels the hurt all over again to have a brother who was not stable psychologically. Jodi shuts the album.

"Those times are gone," he says, "and now all I can do is hope and pray I get a chance to raise my son."

Several weeks into the month of September, the public defender contacts Jodi; the papers are in. The psychiatrist released the records for court of law to both attorneys assigned to the McCain case. Jodi braces himself for what he might hear. The good evidence is that Clayton did not make the claim to be Jodi until he was due to be released; his excuse for not having mentioned being innocent earlier was that he was protecting his brother. "He deserved to be protected," he stated to Barbara McConnell, "but through you I learn that I matter, too."

Jodi thinks about their father and mother; he searches through his memories at the times Clayton was in trouble and how their father attempted to beat the behavior out of him. "I wish you were more like your brother," their mother would say and "I have only one son," was often her wishes. Jolene turns back to the boxes; there must be something useful in there. In the one bedroom condo they are cramped, and Jolene doesn't have the space to empty the boxes like she had at home. With the money they received from insurance they think about hiring another attorney to represent them; Jolene mentions

Attorney Michael Davis who Dillon spoke highly about. Once she gets his number she forwards the information to Jodi who makes the call to schedule the appointment for a free consultation. Dillon was a prosecuting attorney and now she thinks highly of defenders especially for those who are wrongly accused as she feels Jodi must be in the right. The public defender was able to secure a three week postponement for the gathering of evidence and Jodi feels that relief. Jolene sits down upon the bed and gathers early school work the boys had done and there in red paint is the handprint of red leaves like a great maple tree staring back at her and she screams.

"It's yours she says. It has your name on it. You must have been in kindergarten," she yelps. In the red paint are the fine details of circles embossed on skin: a legible hand print from the one and only Jodi McCain. She tidies her belongings and phones Adam and then Michael Davis; this time she leaves her name – Jolene Conroy, widow of Dillon Conroy. He responds fairly quickly to her call and she schedules to see him within the next two hours.

"I'm out of court today," he says, "so today is a good time."

Jolene and Jodi leave the condo in route to see Michael when she notices she's being pulled over.

"I wasn't speeding," she says when a uniformed officer approaches her car.

"Ma'am," he says, "I pulled you over after I got a call that this vehicle is stolen."

"Stolen?"

"Do you have license and registration?"

"Yes, I do …," and she retrieves her license only to find that her registration is no longer in the glove compartment.

"Clayton must have taken it out."

"I'm afraid that if you cannot show proof of registration I'm going to have to take you in until all this gets straightened out."

Jolene does not argue. She knows better. She goes willingly to the officer's patrol car and the officer spots the ankle bracelet Jodi is wearing, "I'm afraid I have to take you in as well, sir."

"I'm Officer McCain," Jodi says, but the Officer outside the vehicle doesn't look amused. "Save it for the judge," he says, and Jodi is put inside the vehicle alongside Jolene.

"It's my car," she tries to say from behind the wire frame that protects them.

"I'm just doing my job," he says. When the tow truck lifts her car and takes off, they speed away toward the station and she was not able to make a phone call to the attorney they are going to miss. Inside the station Jolene fumes over the fact the handprint of Jodi's childhood artwork is not in her purse and tucked it away in the back seat. She stands in a cell among other women waiting for the chance to prove the car is her own vehicle – if the title didn't burn in the fire. Jolene contacts Vicki with her single phone call. Vicky goes to the DMV on her behalf to request a title as there is no lien holder. She requests the pertinent documents be faxed to the public defender who can release Jodi. The DMV simply sends a registration and Jolene is released. It takes hours longer but then Jodi can be released and he takes his truck to the impound lot. Jolene gets her car back, but they have missed their appointment with the attorney Michael Davis. At the lot, Jolene is distraught when the impound attendant states, "You were just here." Surely they mean Clayton and not Jodi.

"He's absolutely crazy," she screams, and Jodi tries to console her.

Not only is her registration missing, and her title burned, but the car has been wiped clean; she has no print to link Jodi with his own childhood fingerprints. She feels defeated and Clayton is nowhere to be found until he's sabotaging his twin brother and his pregnant fiancée. She takes it personally and feels the effects of hatred Jodi must be feeling. When they return to the condo after hours spent in a jail cell, Jodi finds his front door left open.

"He's made keys…," Jodi says and Jolene stands in the open hallway as Jodi checks inside.

"He's gotten to the boxes," he says from inside. "He's taken everything…," he says when Jolene feels a breath upon her neck.

"It's me, Jo," he says, and she turns to find Clayton wearing a suit. "I just left court," he says and he extends his hand to her, "you have to believe me … Clayton has convinced himself he's me."

Jolene doesn't flinch. "Clayton, I'm sorry …" she

begins…

"No, Jo, it's me. He's got you confused."

His face is earnest. Saddened.

Jodi emerges, "He's taken…" is all he says, when he finds Clayton standing over Jolene and she is nervous but astute.

"Yes, Jodi," she says and she takes his side, "I know it's you." Jodi looks perplexed.

"Jolene," his demeanor is cautious.

"No." She says, "I'm with him." And she takes his hands into hers, "We are leaving," she continues, "don't try to follow us."

"He's completely delusional, Jo…"

And she silences his pleading with a slight wave as she walks away and allows Clayton to take her by the hand. He takes her to the hotel where he has been staying. She accompanies him with a deep breath and a hand around his arm.

"You must believe me," he says, "I want to take care of you and the baby…"

"I know," she says, and he removes his suit jacket and tie.

"My lawyer says I have a real good chance to prove I'm innocent of what he did to me by proving I am who I say I am."

"You're Jodi. Not Clayton..."

"Yes, Jo. It's me."

"You have to prove you are who you say you are."

"I will," his eyes are a shade of red and his face is flush, "I can with your help."

"How can I help you?"

"You know my mother. She told you I am who I say I am."

"The birthmark?"

"Momma used to say it was Texas."

"She only wanted you."

"That's why he lies. He's lying to you, Jo. He's not who he says he is."

"How can I help you prove it?"

"You know the truth. You know I am who I say I am."

"You stole my journals?"

"That was him. Not me." He takes her by the hand and down on one knee.

"He killed Kimberly."

She feels a pain in her stomach like a knife.

"Dillon always said…"

"Who killed Kimberly?" He looks earnest. "And that was my brother, Clayton, but he took my name and he became a cop... but he killed her. He is the one who belongs in jail..."

Jolene knows she only wrote of Dillon in her journals. "Dillon never told me..."

"Never told you what?"

"Who killed Kimberly."

"A psychic doesn't know everything."

And she feels cornered... how does he know? And she thinks he must have been following her.

"Dillon wanted to surprise me on my fortieth birthday...," she begins to shed a tear of hope.

"Surprise you in Montana...," he says. But no, she knows for certain she only wrote in her journal... "A trip to Montana," she says, "to renew our vows and he played my favorite song on the radio..."

She knows she has never spoken of Dillon and Jodi would never know.

"What song was it?"

"November Rain," he says and she cries. "Why that song?"

"Because together in November you lost the baby."

She chokes and he squeezes her hand .... He has read her journals. And she puts her head upon his shoulder and

234

she sobs. "But I've never told anyone…," she whispers in his ear.

"You told me."

"No. You're wrong. I never told Jodi." She says and Clayton is incorrect… she and Dillon never told anyone and their secrets were only written among her journals – those journals she meant to make a memoir. And Jodi would not have known.

"You read my journals," she says, and he becomes furious.

"You told me…," he says and her hands shake.

And she turns to leave when his hands grasp around her ankle and he pulls her down and she falls hard to the floor – she wonders if he'll let go if all he wants is for her to agree he's Jodi and so she says, "Jodi, please let go." And his hands grow tighter and the night grows darker.

Chapter Twenty

Clayton slides his hand up her skirt as he gravitates toward her abdomen.

"I'll just reach inside you right here and pull that out," his other hand reaches in between the mattress and the box spring and withdrawals a handgun. He points the barrel toward her temple when the door knob turns; Jodi uses a key because the manager cannot tell them apart. Clayton is a spitting image of Jodi down to the close shave.

"You don't want her," he says. Jodi notices the silence on his pistol.

"You're right, brother," Clayton says as he stands to his feet and kicks her feet toward Jodi as Jodi advances to shield her body Clayton sends off one round that misses them both and a second that grazes his shoulder; on the third, Clayton gets his chest. Jodi is on the ground grimacing.

"Fool me once, shame on me. Fool me twice shame on you." He laughs.

"You never had me fooled," Jodi lets out a sound of pain.

Jolene cowers beneath his body as his blood stains his shirt.

"I fooled that little wife of yours once or twice," Clayton is menacing. His eyes grow black with pupils that look deranged.

With his feet he removes Jodi's body from on top of Jolene.

"We can leave him to die here or we can take him to the cemetery now."

He laughs in his harrowing voice, "I'm not up for any charges," he laughs again, "Just need to prove I'm innocent being you." He spits. The ground is wet. Jodi gazes at Jolene as the light begins to blur his vision as he loses blood.

"You're confused," Jolene says, "if you're Jodi then that means you killed Kimberly. He's being charged with first degree murder."

"Pity you never made it to the attorney."

His voice grumbles. "Plans have changed." He picks her up off the floor.

"Now, kitty-cat, I'm leaving with you here tonight and you're going to tell all your little friends that I'm your man and my name is Jodi ... play along, Clayton lives. Don't play along and he gets buried here tonight."

"If I play along then he goes to jail."

"Wow," his armed hand flails about, "You're quick sweetheart."

"Now, we go to the hospital with the dying Mr. Clayton and get him all fixed up. He's going to sign a plea bargain or else he gets life in prison. You see how this works?"

"Yes."

"And if my brother here doesn't comply then you and that little bun in the oven will drown in the pool. An accident, of course."

"You have this well thought out."

"Well now, Jo-Jo. You slip on the water and crack your head open you see …"

"Do I now?"

"Don't be smart…"

"Jo, just listen to him."

"She will if she wants you to live."

"The story here tonight is honest Abe the peace officer shot his brother here in self-defense. I go free and you will rot in prison with all those friends of yours… I'm sure they'll remember you putting them away like street trash."

"You weren't street trash…"

Clayton becomes irate, "I wasn't now was I?" He hollers, before thinking, and he points the pistol to her abdomen,

"Pick up the phone and dial 911. You will tell them Jodi has shot Clayton… and sound believable or the two of you die and don't think I won't throw your bodies in the river."

"I thought I'd drown in the pool…"

As her words come out he grabs her by the face and forces the weapon to her mouth. "Then we're going out to the pool," and he ushers her body out the door.

"No!" Jodi screams. "Clayton!"

"Wrong response," Clayton hollers as he stomps Jodi's face onto the Berber carpet.

"I'll make the call," Jolene says but Clayton's face has turned to crimson and he sweats profusely.

"You had your chance," he grabs her by the hair and walks her onto the balcony; he forces her abdomen into the railing and she leans over the edge, "I can push you over right now." He holds the revolver to the back of her head when someone approaches.

"Hey, are you all right?" A masculine voice says and Clayton puts an arm over her shoulder and the barrel to her back.

"Tell him how you're doing, sweetheart."

"I'm fine," she says as she now considers her baby.

"You have any more you want to say to me?" He whispers.

"Are you sure?" The man says and Jolene nods. "I'm okay," she says, and Clayton directs her to the room.

"Because of you," his menacing voice says, "we can just stay here and watch him die. He'll bleed out for sure."

"No," she says, "I'm sorry," her voice shakes, "I'll

say what you want."

Clayton gleams as he takes a seat on the bed and pulls his feet up.

He rests his back on the headboard and Jolene picks up the phone. She makes the call.

As Jodi is transported on the gurney, Clayton gives a full report.

"My brother is delusional," he says, and the EMT takes a note alongside the police, "He stole my identity you see, when we were just kids. My brother is Clayton pretending to be Jodi. He lied and they put me in jail. Tonight he tried to shoot me."

"Where is his gun?" The officer asks as Clayton pulls a pistol from beneath the bed.

"He must have taken my gun…," Jodi whispers to Jolene, but she ushers him into the ambulance. "Don't say anymore," she says, and the EMT pulls the doors closed and she is left with the officers.

"So you're saying you are Jodi McCain?"

"Yes sir. Yes I am. Always have been."

In the hospital the surgical team works vigorously for hours to remove the bullet that has entered Jodi's chest and lodged behind his spine. The doctors are not yet certain if he will walk again. Jolene gives a report to the officer and she contends that Jodi is who he says he is and that Clayton is criminal. The officer files both statements and leaves for the office where he will file a report. Jolene sits in the waiting room as her baby kicks from within her abdomen thinking that his father's fate is not certain. She wonders how Clayton would have gotten into Jodi's safe and believes he must be hiring others to track him… and she contends further that Clayton isn't working alone. She phones Adam to learn if he can track Clayton as opposed to Jodi.

"If I don't get them mixed up," Adam says feeling the nightmare she must be experiencing. When they end the call she feels some relief knowing that her own private investigator could turn tricks by tracking the other side of the conflict. Clayton has viciously turned Jodi's life upside down – if he lives. *He must live*, she says aloud to no one who is there when she phones Vicky instead of her sister because she doesn't want to cause her stress.

"Hello?" Vicky says.

"It's me, Vic," Jolene says.

"I saw your name come up, what's happening?"

"I'm at the hospital," she says and she tells Vicky of the happenings of the past two hours. Vicky listens tentatively, "I wish you could get away from all that." She knows ultimately that it's all true – one brother, even if she doesn't know which one, is delusional.

"I do believe Clayton is deceptive if not delusional," Jolene voices, "and if I hang in there I might be able to prove it."

"Or get killed." Vicky is frank.

Several hours later the doctor emerges. "We were able to

avoid his spine," Doctor Fitzgerald says, "and we successfully removed the bullet. He's in some pain but should regain his balance. The bullet did damage to some surrounding nerves but he should regain feeling." Jolene thanks him and she is permitted to see Jodi who has not awoken from anesthesia. She brushes her fingers through his short hair and takes a deep breath. She wants the nightmare to be over. She pulls her rain jacket over her shoulder and peers at the deluge outside the window. It is October and she was to be getting married; not only has she not married, but she's lost some photo clients for their big day - she's astounded by their refusal to interact with her based on Clayton's behavior – or is this all a wakeup call? She tries to dismiss the idea but she dwells on the facts thinking that all of this could have been avoided if Dillon were alive – or is she just feeling sorry for herself? Her mind continues to ruminate on the past and she thinks too that Kimberly would be alive… her flighty, pay no attention to the rules, roommate, if it wasn't for her. She blames herself and falls asleep. During sleep she is faced with Clayton who aims his gun directly to her forehead when she flinches and wakes up. Only thirty minutes has gone by and she gets a drink of water. *Vicky is right,* she ponders aloud in the mirror as though she can barely recognize herself. She splashes water onto her face and as the nurse walks in Jodi wakes up.

She wants him to know that she is near and she holds his hand. He is getting fluids from an IV but the nurse encourages him to try to eat when he can. He nods and she inserts the pain meds into his port. His back is sensitive from the nerve damage and he grimaces. Within twenty minutes he's back asleep without having said a word. Jolene leaves in the early dawn and enters the wet

242

streets. She sends a text to Adam for an update but he has yet to respond. She goes back to the condo. Back to anything else she can find; as she tears through the boxes she ravishes bits of paper as if with a strong declaration of her intention there is something within them that can be delivered to the court system that will reveal he is Jodi McCain and innocent of all charges. She cuts each taped box with a knife until she finds art projects, the second one in the box, and she removes thirty year old papier-mâché and finds prints stamped in glue. The name on the bottom is Clayton McCain written in early elementary writing without uppercase letters. She digs more – if only to find something else and there are among shards of paper some drawings, photos and early Christmas ornaments made of clay; one for each boy with a footprint like a sarcophagus. She takes the clay and the glue yielding a thumb print in rubber cement and exits the condo when she bumps shoulders with a large sandy brown colored man whose long hair hasn't been washed beneath a tight fitting bandana. She makes haste down the stairs and avoids the elevator feeling that Clayton is on to her and she rounds the corner to the outside when she thinks of the public defender being her only hope at the last minute when something from nowhere shatters before her face and she's knocked unconscious.

She awakes bound and tied. She's gagged on the bandana she saw earlier. She's sickened. When the trunk opens it's nearing sunset and she can barely breathe. The man she saw is now facing her.

"He told me to tell you he'd drown you in a river."

He lifts her from the trunk and drags her bound body to

the dock. She feels her baby inside her when her cell phone rings and he notices they are not alone; "Hey there," a familiar voice says, she finds Adam walking towards them when the burly man turns away and yields a knife. With his right hand, he thrusts toward Adam who moves swiftly like being on air; he is skilled in martial arts and he suspends the huge man's arm behind his back but he's powerful and escapes his grip when Adam throws a leg and spins into a roundhouse side kick; he goes down and is knocked unconscious.

Adam quickly goes to a pregnant Jolene. "I had to track you," he says, "it's a protocol I use on all my clients. I'm sorry I couldn't tell you." And he removes the bandana that bounds her mouth. When he slips it off, she lets out a howling cry. Her tears pour from her vacant eyes, "I can't do this anymore," she says into his shoulder, "I can't take any more of this shit," she hollers in half anger and the rest remorse.

"I know," he says, "I understand, and you must realize now this is why I track all my clients because they put out a hit on you."

Jolene is still sullen. "I just want to know that the father of my baby is an innocent man," she wipes her face with a free hand as he removes the knots that bound her wrist.

"I'm working on it, trust me I'm trying to help you."

"Well of course... you just saved my life!" She is breathing heavily.

"You're not the first. Your life is part of my job."

"Makes sense." She musters a half smile, "Without

me you don't get paid."

"That's right," he smiles back, "you're no good to me dead."

He walks her to his Mercedes and she slides into the back seat as the first police cruiser arrives because he makes the call. Sergeant Harris takes her statement as Officer O'Neil cuffs and apprehends the large, overbearing man who she learns is Sedgwick Malcolm Jones – a hitman by trade with the guise of a street rider and motorcycle mechanic. Jodi tells Adam of the prints she collected that day and Officer Harris searches the car. They search the condo. This information means a lot to Jolene – a now personal agenda – and Adam knows that. After hours of indirection, Sergeant Harris and Officer O'Neil find the childhood memories thrown into the dumpster out back after they swipe the local grounds for any evidence that will help a fellow police officer.

"The precinct is still rooting for you," Officer O'Neil says, and their forensics specialist dusts for prints and snaps shots of the evidence.

In the hospital Jodi is awake. Jolene is taken to the hospital to be reviewed and they check the baby with a sonogram; to her relief he is not affected by the stress, she does have a concussion and from the evidence they find in Jolene's vehicle they can attest she was assaulted with a crowbar that is used for opening locked cars. She is given medication for the pain and is told if she experiences seizures she would be given more medication for the symptoms. She does not have blood clots or other obstructions and would be sensitive to light for the next several weeks until the concussion subsides.

The medical staff wheel Jolene into Jodi's room and they are placed side-by-side. Jodi takes one look at her eyes searching for how she can still love him.

"I'm sorry," he says, and he cannot look away; he searches for her insatiable devotion to him — even when he thought he should let her go — because she was too special in his eyes to put up with criminal behavior, but Jolene is a rare gem. She not only stays but she risks her life to put the man behind bars that jeopardizes the health of her family. She has lost clients, her home, at times her sanity, and her ability to trust — but she puts that trust back into Jodi because he gives to her something she was to never have. And she thinks more about her baby and less about Clayton, and when her phone chimes she receives a text: *You're lying with the one who put the hit out on you.* She turns over with her back to Jodi and with a pain in her side she believes she has her first contraction.

Chapter Twenty-One

I'm in the delivery room, her sister sends her a text as Jolene nurses her baby on her chest. There is an Officer outside her door. Jodi cannot be in the maternity ward; he is still recovering from a bullet lodged in his back. Vicky brings her a cup of coffee. Jolene has received messages from Clayton, who the police are currently searching for. The forensic specialists dipped his big toe and index finger in ink. They have made comparisons to the childhood prints; "We ran the prints," Sergeant Harris tells her, "no matter what he says now, we've got the prints to a Jodi McCain and they match Jodi McCain." Sergeant Harris is firm.

"Surprise. Surprise," Officer O'Neil says and walks about the room.

"We're waiting to get a location on him," Sergeant Harris radios the precinct.

Jolene finally responds to her text: *Sis, I'm so happy for you ... is all she can say ... I too went into early labor ... I had Hudson James McCain last night.*

Jolene does not get a response but she feels Henley will be safe and beautiful and now the officers are working to keep her baby alive and well. Hudson has Jodi's eyes and dark hair. There's no doubt he's his daddy but he has an uncle who is unstable, then Jolene hears about the paperwork his attorney received from the psychiatrist; she learns that Clayton has confusion from a diagnosed hemorrhage from within the brain that the medical staff say is from self-inflicted behavior.

"He needs brain surgery." The psychiatrist passes on to the public defender, "our medical staff diagnosed him but he was let go here."

Clayton was otherwise let go because he earned good time and they had no problems with him inside the facility.

"He was a smart kid," one of the medical staff said of him but they believed he was suicidal and hit the ground hard when he jumped from the top stair.

"And they didn't believe he fell," the public defender passes to the Officer. Jolene overheard some of his conversation and inquires.

"He had a fall?" She's mildly curious only because she wants it to be over.

"Attempted suicide." The Officer is unshaded, "Jumped off a balcony. Needs brain surgery from a concussion. A brain hemorrhage."

Serves him right, Jolene thinks but she says nothing.

"Too bad for that," Vicky pipes in.

"What's that?" Jolene says gazing at her now sleeping son's sleeping face.

"That he wasn't successful." She sniggers.

"That would have been too easy," Jolene says.

"Can you believe they succeeded though?"

"Who?"

"The forensics?"

"That's them."

"He was saved by a big toe," Jolene chimes.

"Well, thank God for that... and for you," she taps Jolene's shoulder, "by the sound of things he was giving up."

"He felt powerless."

"Probably for the first time in his life."

"His life was in shambles."

In the next moment Jolene beams as Jodi is wheeled into the room.

"He is strong," Vicky says and she stands to let him in, "I'll go get a refill on my coffee," she says and leaves the room to let them get time alone.

He leans over her and kisses his son on the head, "How are you feeling, Jo?"

"I'm fine," she says, "Gwynn is in delivery today."

"Is she early?"

"Two weeks."

"October babies are fun... think of all the Halloween parties."

"You're right."

The nurse checks his lines to be sure he's getting the medication. "It's impressive really," she says sweetly, "how well you're doing."

"Thank you," Jodi says and he takes his son into his arms. Jolene snaps a photo and hits send then she waits to hear from her sister again. She doesn't let go of the moment and takes another photo when her own nurse walks in, "Would you like me to take a photo of the three of you?"

"Yes," Jolene says in unison.

The nurse takes a succession of photos and they thank her.

Twelve hours into the night she is awoken by her sister who sends a photo and a message: *Congratulations, Sis, but what happened to … is it Jodi?*

Yes, she responds … *Jodi was shot, Gwynn … I didn't want to alarm you. Clayton hired someone to attack us.* She messages the best way she can. *But please don't worry. We're okay now.*

Jolene??? Her sister is speechless.

Yes, I know. Right now we're trying to avoid anymore media.

Outside a journalist has asked for a statement but the officers block their interference. Jodi has made the front cover of the paper before and they hope to cover him again. The media has learned of the incident via police scanners and await an official statement. Jolene is in no hurry to leave the hospital until she gets another message from her sister: *Jo, I want you well. Jack and I have a surprise for you.*

She wonders what her sister is up to.

A surprise?

No worries, her sister responds and she sends her sister a heart.

We need to visit soon.

When you're well, Jo. Your life has become news stories!!

I know, Gwynn.

It's scary, Jo.

Yes. I'm sorry.

You're not the one who should be sorry.

He is sorry, Gwynn.

Who?

Jodi.

I meant Clayton.

He's sick … he suffered a brain trauma. Attempted suicide.

Don't stick up for him.

I'm not. It's just the truth.

But how are you? He physically hurt you?

Yes. But I'm okay now.

They end their messages with hugs and love when Jolene receives another message.

251

You're with the wrong brother, he sends followed by a skull with crossbones and as he texts he is tracked by the police.

Jodi is taken back to his room to await discharge orders – but he will receive physical therapy from an outpatient clinic.

Jolene is in the hospital for three days following her cesarean. Hudson is healthy and strong despite being five weeks early. She is tickled to have a baby at the same time as her sister. They were always so close; now the cousins can have a similar relationship. But there is fear on her mind too – what is Clayton to do next?

"He's mentally unstable," she tells Jodi as she helps him to tie his shoes.

"He has you helping me to tie my shoes," Jodi says, "I don't want you alone," his voice cracks and he breaks, "what the hell am I to do if I lose you?"

She holds his head in her arms and when she places the baby in his car seat they are ushered out the door with the police accompanying them. They are led outside where the media surrounds them. "Officer McCain, were you shot by your own twin brother?" A journalist pursues them. "Has he been found?" Another says.

But he dodges their inquiries.

"Out of the hospital, and into the court room," Jodi says the following day. He is bound to a wheel chair while he does outpatient physical therapy. The court presides and Jodi's attorney reveals to the court documentation explaining that a twin brother is currently being reviewed for identity theft and has been claiming to be her client. The judge overhears their case and while Clayton is a no-show, Jodi's case is put on a stet docket while they file a case against Clayton McCain for the death of Kimberly. Jolene reflects again how Dillon knew someone was to kill a woman by the name of Kimberly; in that respect, she thinks it's as if Dillon is having this experience with her. She feels relief when the public defender uses the birth prints with his current day prints; then they only need to prove Clayton claimed Jodi's uniforms from dry cleaner and, as she has the thought, the investigator brings out the surveillance from the dry cleaners; but it's as if it's no use because the judge cannot tell them apart. Clayton made a valiant effort to personify Jodi especially with his appearance in uniform; as Jodi became unkempt, so did Clayton. Then she thinks about Sedgwick the hitman who can testify against Clayton as he had been paid to murder both Jolene and Jodi; but that case is being drawn up as the case of first degree murder unfolds; Jodi's team must prove Clayton is a fraud and turn the case over to preside in a new case. Jodi is tired but relieved temporarily with the stet docket; he knows now that he must once again testify against his own brother just as he had done when they were school children. For being twins, the two of them had never been close. Jolene learns too, on the day of court, that Jodi received detention for his brother's loud outbursts that caused their arguments in class. Jolene must wait until the end of the court hearing to learn what that argument must have been about.

In that time, Jolene receives a text from Gwyneth stating she is home with the baby. Jolene is fortunate to have Vicky who is watching Hudson for the day. Gwyneth then writes her sister who says there is a surprise for Jolene when she leaves for the day. Jolene is anxious in the good and the bad way; she yearns to leave with Jodi to begin their lives anew and nervous too about what her sister may have up her sleeve. She feels guilty because her sister does too much. She gathers her belongings after another four hours after Jodi is let go by the court system and is pending a hearing to preside in the case against Clayton who first must be charged and proven to commit fraud before the case can go to trial for first degree murder. Jodi is no stranger to testifying in the court system and feels the weight and pressure of the pending trial against his brother just as they had done as kids. He feels the burden of having to testify but knows he has taken an oath to uphold the law and first degree murder is taken seriously; he feels he had no choice but to testify then and now. When they return to the condo they find Adam is there to guide them.

"Your sister sought me out to help you," he says, "follow me."

He guides them to a taxi and they climb into the rear seat; the taxi driver has been told where to take them. At the end of their ride they find themselves faced in front of a piece of land and Jolene recognizes Jared.

"Oh, no," she says, feeling awkward.

"What is it?" Jodi is calm after the storm. He really just wants rest. The taxi driver takes his wheelchair from the trunk and Jodi is helped from the taxi.

"What is this?" Jolene asks as Jared approaches them.

"This is a gift from your sister and some friends," he says.

Then Vicky shows up yielding a leash holding an anxious Cash and baby Hudson in his car seat.

"Vicky, what is going on?" Jolene is perplexed.

"Your sister got in touch with me," she explains, "she feels you have been through too much in the last two years since you lost Dillon..." Vicky's voice cracks and she has tears in her eyes, "You may not feel you need it but Gwyneth feels you deserve it ... and I feel you deserve it... this is your land. Your piece of property that has been bought for you."

"Bought for me?" She is astonished.

"Jared here is going to build you a custom made property..."

"Shut the front door!" Jolene is floored.

"It's what the lot of us has done for you."

"There are twelve of us ... Jodi, Gregory and Alayna included, who put together half a million dollars to buy your property, and you get to build a custom made home with Jared's help."

"Jared," Jolene says, "you've been hired to build my house?"

"That's right. Just like Vicky said."

Jolene finally processes it all, and takes Hudson from his car seat and she places her sleeping baby in Jodi's arms.

"I want a picture," Jolene says, "a before and after picture."

They gather together in front of Jolene and Jodi's vacant lot, and Jared takes the photo. Jolene quickly gets on the phone. "Gwynn," she says, "you shouldn't have!" Tears form in her eyes.

"Well, we did!" Gwyneth is happy.

Jolene hugs Jodi and together they kiss for the first time since Clayton got between them. His lips are smooth like glass yet warm despite the chilly weather.

November rolls on by and in December, Jolene makes a crochet Santa suit for the baby's first Christmas. They are not alone but find themselves in Montana where they wish to stay for the month. Jolene and Jodi plan a Christmas wedding, and Jolene tells her current husband that their wedding is on the birthday of her belated husband Dillon who she says was an angel presiding over them. When she tells Jodi of the psychic, he too feels they have to thank him. Jodi is honored to have her on the date of his birth because his life meant peace to Jolene when they were together.

"I hope it's not weird," Jolene says.

"Well, it may be a bit weird," he says, and he stands subtly from his wheelchair to balance momentarily on sturdy legs and they laugh together in that moment. He takes a seat but has been making progress; he will walk again the doctors say, and as she does the home therapy he gains feeling in his feet. They wed at a beautiful lodge by the lake with the snow outside; she feels in awe of the landscape.

"It's so beautiful."

"You're so beautiful," Jodi says.

They have photos taken of their traditional and elegant wedding attire; Jolene is classy in a long sweetheart dress and Jodi wears a light suit and a deep purple vest. Jolene is thankful and as she gazes out the window as she walks the red carpet in front of their close friends and guests, she says a silent thank you to Dillon for being such a splendid husband whose time together she cherishes and then she thanks her sister and friends for being her rock when life grew harsh and unbearable in the face of it all.

She works remotely to help Jared fabricate their home. They settle for both modern and chic with some industrial touches on a modest home. Jolene looks at images of her newly designed studio, and with the insurance payment from their previous home she can replenish what she lost. She thinks about the journals that burned realizing they never told the whole story anyway and it was Dillon's story she wanted to tell and not her own – but perhaps he'd cherish more the secrets of their past that only they held together – without being told, and through Clayton reading those secrets, she has learned a life lesson; not all stories are written but some are bound in memories that are cherished more than a sack of gold – she is now keeping them sacred. Through her new marriage and all she shares with her new husband, she has a new story to tell that does not begin with the predicaments formed by Clayton but with the birth of their son – a story that is worth a thousand words but cannot be written because it is too busy being experienced.

So blessed be.

ABOUT THE AUTHOR

Candace Meredith earned her Bachelor of Science degree in English Creative Writing from Frostburg State University in the spring of 2008. Her works of poetry, photography and fiction have appeared in literary journals Bittersweet, The Backbone Mountain Review, The Broadkill Review, In God's Hands/ Writers of Grace, A Flash of Dark, Greensilk Journal, Saltfront, Mojave River Press and Review, Scryptic Magazine, Unlikely Stories Mark V, The Sirens Call, The Great Void, BAM Writes, Foreign Literary, Lion and Lilac Magazine and various others. Candace lives in Virginia with her son and her daughter, her newborn baby and fiancée. She earned her Master of Science degree in Marketing and Communications from West Virginia University. Candace is the author of various books titled Contemplation: Imagery, sound and Form in Lyricism (a collection of poetry), Losing You (a novella collection), Winter Solstice (book 1 of a 4 book series): The Crone (book 2), The Lady of Brighton (book 3), Summer Solstice (book 4 in progress) and her recently published first children's book A-Hoy Frankie Your Riverboat Captain!

Made in the USA
Middletown, DE
07 May 2022

65103664R00146